I0741513

A Pale Shade of Honor

Carl Mabbs-Zeno

Khotso Publishing
Peterborough, NH

This novel is a work of fiction and not a memoir. Although it utilizes the author's personal experience in some cases, many of the characters and incidents have no specific historical counterpart.

Mabbs-Zeno, Carl C.
  A Pale Shade of Honor / Carl C. Mabbs-Zeno
  ISBN 978-1-7331262-2-9

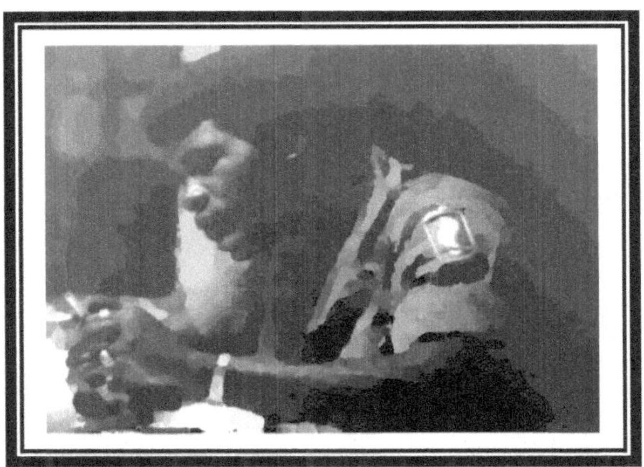

He leaned on the bar while the smoke
from his cigarette curled around his head...

A Pale Shade of Honor

Contents

Introduction

As a child I did not know World War II was recent, that, as a baby-boomer, I was its product in a manner of thinking or, more importantly, that the thinking of my times were dominated by it. To me, it was just the part of history that could see seen on documentary film, albeit black-and-white. As an old man, who finally got around to thinking about World War I on its hundredth anniversary, I find it ironic that World War II was the only war I thought relevant in modern times, except for my own war in Vietnam, and yet World War I probably more profoundly shaped the century in which I grew up and certainly was more similar to my war, as viewed by the soldiers. They both sent out young men to fight without knowing why. The part that makes no sense is that the young men did so willingly in both world wars.

I. Childhood

A male child in the 1950's, like me, expected to face evil with a gun someday and knew it would be his duty to aim true when the moment came. I was introduced to guns at a young age but not in any way serious. Nonetheless. the video gamers of the 21st Century who get carpel tunnel syndrome from shooting for hours at made-up enemies may be no more inured to faux violence than I was with my cap pistols for detective or cowboy personae, battery-operated burp gun for war action, plastic rifle for protection from (not aggression toward) Indians, and water pistol for active simulation of interpersonal violence. The burp gun would have been my favorite toy when I was a certain age, except that I could never find fresh batteries so I toted it around and made my own sounds. The cap pistols had a similar handicap in that they were best when they had caps but I rarely had caps. It was my own fault that I could not keep myself armed. Whenever I had a roll of caps, I hit it with a hammer to get a bigger bang. The faint snap of a single cap was not very satisfying although the scent of what I imagined to be gunpowder was pleasant.

Duck and deer hunting were respectable sports in my rural Pennsylvania community but I did not know anyone who actually did either. I did not like the idea of killing beautiful animals, even if it were needed to replace the natural predators. I might have been swung around if I had any real opportunity to learn to hunt. The closest I came was when my mother cooked up a duck that a hunter had shot too near to the house and not claimed. I had not eaten much of it since it was shared across the six of us in the family, but it seemed extraordinarily exciting to eat from the land. Besides, ducks were pretty common around there in those years.

Still, I was a little jealous of the boys at school whose fathers or uncles hunted and who let them fire a few real rounds from a rifle. I knew better than to wish for a BB gun. The closest I got to firing an actual gun was to push the barrel of a friend's air rifle into the ground to put a clot of dirt in the end and then fire it out in a gritty puff that went no more than a couple feet.

I was introduced to patriotism in a casual way, not like the formal instruction and active indoctrination I experienced into the church. Mainly, I remember that the flag was considered very special. We hung it on the screen

porch for the Fourth of July one year and I wondered why
we did not have it up more often. I supposed it was because
it was put away someplace where we could not find it again,
but that probably reflects my level of disorganization rather
than my parents'.

II. High School

My high school years seemed extraordinarily
ordinary to me. Maybe that is a common impression
among young people, people for whom their own lives are
most of what they know of the world. In truth, I had a very
common experience for my time and place although it was
much privileged relative to, say, most youths in South Africa,
or Bridgeport, Connecticut.

My greatest pleasure was in tramping through the
woods. My mother gave me the impression this form of
enjoyment was to be admired so I felt pride in it. Socially, I
had all the friends I wanted in number, although I would
have liked it better if at least one of them had been female.

I did not like school but I tolerated it and it
tolerated me with my better-than-average grades and less-
than-average effort (at an age when low effort in school was
widespread). My reputation among the boys, and my
singular passion, was founded in wrestling. It was not the
most popular sport at our school but doing well in it carried
weight. I was too skinny to look athletic but I was actually
quite good at wrestling in my rangy way. At this sport, I
worked harder than in all my classes combined.

Adults, and probably girls, thought I was smart, not
athletic. I had an effective way of looking adults in the eye,
including teachers and not including girls. I tired of being

termed an "underachiever," although, of course, not so much as to do anything about it.

The Vietnam War became an American issue when I was in high school, but mostly for the intellectual kids who worked on the school paper. I did not know much about it and it did not affect me in any way I noticed. By the spring of 1965, when I was a junior, it had a reputation within my milieu as an unfortunate and inglorious affair that needed to be avoided. But it was also the biggest thing going and I worried that it would be over before I got to college where I could join the peace movement. In that year, an alumnus of my high school was killed in Vietnam. There was an announcement over the school public address system. I did not know him but I knew his sister slightly, that is, I knew who she was. She was older than me and went to our church. Everyone seemed very sympathetic toward her. There was a page in the yearbook that year dedicated to her brother. Those two references to him, the PA announcement and the yearbook page, were the only official mentions of the war that I heard in my high school. The subject was never raised by any teacher in my presence. Similarly, I do not think my parents ever mentioned it to me until I was about to be drafted. Sure, it was famously on the evening news every night, but I was allowed to watch television only on weekends and rarely saw the news. I did not read the newspaper except the Sunday funnies. My friends did not speak of it; we were too young for it to be personally relevant and the issues were over our heads, although I was dimly aware it might be relevant to me someday.

I hated sentences that began with "society should" and distrusted the sincerity of people who spoke such sentences. Hypocrisy was my biggest moral issue; *Portrait of the Artist as a Young Man*, my exemplar.   Institutions were empty and did not deserve obedience. This stance was a handy substitute for commitment toward anything more significant than wrestling. I expected and awaited an ethical foundation to be discovered in college.

III. College

There was a rumor that you could tell if you were accepted by how thick the envelope was when you heard back from the schools where you had applied. There came a day when those envelopes began to arrive. I had applied to three schools. The first envelop was thick. It was from the state college, my safety school, and I was accepted; no surprise but reassuring anyway. A couple days later the envelope came from the school I had found through my research, the right school for me. It was thin and it rejected me. That was disappointing.

I reserved any emotional response until I heard from my third application, the one to a first tier school I probably should not have considered except that it might let me in since both my parents had gone there. I knew the campus from visits to see football games, the only sporting events my parents ever attended. From these excursions, I knew the stadium, the student union, the library, the ice cream store at the dairy, the arts-and-sciences quad, my father's fraternity house, and the stories that both parents told when we visited those hallowed grounds. It was a great school and a step beyond my reach although I might have been able to handle it if I applied myself. I did not regret having been a poor high school student; my performance level had come to me so naturally I could only accept is as who I was.

A thick envelope eventually arrived. I did not savor the likely implications, but ripped it open as soon as I spotted it on the table in the front hall. I was in. I had succeeded! I was in the right school. Those underachieving grades were good enough. It was my fate to succeed without effort!

It would be hard for college to meet the high expectations my parents and teachers and public literature had built into me for the experience. I anticipated seeing and playing sports, meeting girls, joining a fraternity that would accompany me through life, and learning a profession. In my first days, it all seemed possible. The fall weather was just as it ought to be, cool and bright. Before classes began, freshman orientation told us how to get around campus and signed us up for clubs. The boys in the dorm were a friendly bunch, generally similar to myself. I fit in. Those people who said I needed to work more in high school had been wrong!

Those first days on campus were heady times. It did not feel like a new experience so much as the happy fulfillment of destiny. In our first week, we did not have classes. Our time was devoted to learning our way into the new environment. I was not among those who discovered drinking and I watched with awe those who were so foolish, coming to the dorm in a stupor and puking in the hallway and waking with a hangover as if no one had discovered these things before. I felt slightly superior. My presumptive knowledge was more valuable than their experience in this area.

With the self-confidence that accumulated in those first days, I thought it would be wise to devise a memorable prank that might establish me as a leader across the freshman class. I would like a leader of these fellows. The clock tower above the library was the most conspicuous symbol of the university so my fantasies began there. How could I color the clock face without damaging it and get away with it and be known for having done it? ...Maybe an orange hue to follow a Halloween theme in time for that day. If only I had the skills to climb the stone tower and the chemical knowledge to devise a temporary colorant, I would do it. But I was no longer in high school where I accepted the momentum of my surroundings and I took the challenge a step

further. I went up the hill to look more closely at the clock tower. There was a roof that hit about halfway up. I could sit a ladder on the peak and reach the face of the clock on one side. And when reaching it became feasible in my mind, I had my greatest insight. A peace sign! I could be political! A freshman and already a political figure on campus! Duct tape would do it without harming the clock. I could sign it on one side with broad magic marker, a signature visible from the ground. I would have to sign it with a nickname, a name that would be recognizable as me without getting me arrested. It was brilliant! If only I had a recognized nickname... I could not solve that last part of the scheme and soon abandoned the whole project, but I had been close to fame on my first try.

IV: Culture

Before college, I had listened to the radio only in the car. Not having a car myself, I did not often control which station played, but I did identify strongly with the music of the times. When I rode in my friends' cars or their parents' cars, we always played the popular radio stations. I admired how some of the guys could bounce from station to station, most using the radio presets, to find a particular song. The top songs were played constantly. Motown was the best. The Four Seasons and the Beach Boys were good in their day. We didn't listen to Dylan; the whole folk scene was for a slightly older crowd. I would have liked jazz, I thought, but it was not on the radio, not on the stations we played.

In the first week of college, the campus radio station was ubiquitous: in the cafeteria, the student union, the lounge in the dorm and the clock radio beside my bed. We did not have Walkmen or IPODs to carry it further. In my second week, i.e., after freshman orientation, there was an announcement on the radio that a demonstration was developing in front of the Student Union, just as I anticipated would occur soon. The lounge in the dorm emptied as we all ran up the Hill to be part of whatever it was. It was hard to figure out what was happening. The few fellows I knew had come from the dorm like me with no idea how the thing had begun. There was a line of charter buses along the road by the Union surrounded by a huge, disorganized crowd milling about. No one had any signs; there were no speeches through bull horns. I could hear some angry arguing somewhere near the front of the buses so I worked my way into the crowd. I got close enough to see that some students were lying on the road in front of the buses, blocking them from departing. This looked courageous. The driver of the first bus was inching forward while another driver stood beside the bus and waved him on. Meanwhile the students inside the bus were shouting at their driver and various factions in the crowd tried to make their points. But most of the crowd was merely watching excitedly, like myself. I sorted through the shouts and realized the heroes under the bus were "jocks" who wanted the buses to abandon the trip to Washington for an anti-war protest. Two sides of my self-image faced a confrontation: did I favor the athletes who had, as a class, attracted my family to this campus for several years and whose ranks I aspired to join, or did I favor the students going to Washington? I had not realized there would be any students who supported the War. Our generation was uniformly opposed, wasn't it? The ones on the ground seemed like the innovators, something I did not expect from the jocks. I briefly imagined lying on the pavement beside them. There was no danger except to the first few, the ones nearest the tires. They were being tugged out of the way although I could not see if it was friends or foes pulling them to safety. I also could not imagine that the bus drivers would actually run over anyone. They were surely not taking a political stand one way or the other. The reason the bus could creep forward was that the front row of blockers was constantly retreating out of the way. Ten minutes after I arrived at the front of the crowd, the lead bus had worked its way entirely past me and the protest was falling apart. The jocks had not been as courageous as I thought they ought to be. If they believed in their position, they should have stuck to it; called the bluff of the drivers. Of course, the people on the ground were probably not generally student-athletes; that was simply a characterization from the crowd to describe people supportive of the status quo. My first demonstration had been pro-war. College would be even more interesting than I had hoped.

V: Girls

In that first week, the most serious task before me was to find a girl. The girls in college were all my age or older which was a huge change from high school where they had all been my age or younger. There were attractive girls everywhere; surely one would be looking for me.

The resident advisor from in my dorm set up a mixer on our second evening, having called a resident advisor in one of the girls' dorms. There were fifty or so guys on my floor, nearly all of whom went to the mixer in the lounge of the girls' dorm. Like most of the guys, I wore a sport coat over a sweater and felt years older than I was at my high school prom. They served an alcoholic punch that was legal for 18-year-olds in New York State but I was still 17 by a month. The situation was very positive and entirely new to me yet I was my familiar self and did not know what to do or, if I did, I lacked the guts to do it. After only one day at school, I did not know any of the guys and they did not know each other and that was all right for them. I was used to being around boys I did not know, but it left me without a base of conversation. So I stood around wondering if anything was going to happen, like music or some welcoming speeches.

There were about fifty girls at the event as well, a disappointing lot. There were five or six who looked interesting to me. If any of them came up to me and started a conversation, it would have been all right. The six were not on their own for long and none of them ever gave a glance in my direction. A couple fellows brought a girl over to me and whispered that I ought to talk to her. They were entirely well intentioned, but the basis for their selection was that she was too tall for a regular guy and I was the tallest guy on our floor. I had not noticed being the tallest. I felt like screaming "Don't you see she's taller than me too!" but that would have done no good.

I saw their logic; she was what I deserved. Apart from being tall, she was big, neither fat nor slim, just a big girl all around. I was skinny and not a good match for her physically. Her face was not bad, but not particularly good either. She showed no style. I guessed she was smart. This was, apart from myself, a school full of high achievers. We gave each other our names and went on to mention our hometowns. I do not remember any further conversation although I did stand next to her for a long time. On the way back to our dorm, someone asked me if I was going to see her again. It had not occurred to me to ask her.

The next week I saw the "pig book" for the first time. It had a picture of all the freshmen and a short summary of each person's background. It was a good idea for helping freshmen meet people but it was in fact used only, as far as I could tell, to assess the girls. My own entry used my high school yearbook photo. It was as good a picture as I had of myself, but it was not good enough that any cool girl would look me up and give me try. It was good for us sitting in the lounge to tell each other who we liked and what we would say if we saw them.

While I was engaged in this group fantasy, someone came in and said I had a phone call... from a girl. I thought it would have to be my mother but it turned out to be from a girl who had gone to my high school and was now here at this school. She found me in the pig book. I remembered hearing she had gone to school here, but it had not been significant to me. She suggested we get together for a drink at one of the student hang-out bars. She was not an unappealing girl. I might have spoken to her once or twice in high school, not in a personal conversation but something like "Has the late bus left yet?" I could not imagine why she would be so kind as to go out with me. All I could think was that she was a year older than me and Jewish. I was not sure why I was so conscious of her being Jewish, just that I would have expected her to be interested in Jewish boys, which was generally irrelevant at the moment since she was not interested in me, just being exceptionally polite and generous. I explained that I did not know the bar she mentioned and she said she would meet me at my dorm. When I left the phone in the hallway, someone asked if I made a date and I had to say "yes," that someone from my high school was coming over. The lounge emptied as guys came out to congratulate me. Of course those in the group that had been reviewing the pig book were not the ones most likely to have dates.

Isabel came by. We stood in the hallway and talked for nearly thirty minutes. She told me what she liked about college. I did not explain I was under-age for going to a bar and after some time I said I needed to get back to my room. She knew I was not rejecting her, that I was just too inept to even consider a date with her, or even the cordial get-together she had proposed well short of a date. I admired her for her sophistication and hoped I would be capable of more when I was a sophomore.

Meeting a girl should not have been hard, they were all around us, but getting a word beyond the opening greeting never came to me as a freshman. I did not want to get started with a girl who was not good looking enough and I did not feel any girl who was good looking would get started with me, a story too common to tell. So I cannot more fully explain any more of the day I gestured to the open seat beside me when a lovely girl came into class and she nodded to me and took the seat. No words were spoken, you see. That night, I looked her up in the pig book and found her name and phone number. That is as far as it got although I kept her name in reserve in case I needed to dream of concretely meeting a girl. I was not in a rush. College would last four years. Later I would be more familiar with things and more confident.

None of the guys around me had found a girl. The guys I knew were either wrestlers, and too busy for girls, or the card players in the dorm with personalities as shy as mine, at least with females. We were very outgoing among each other. The card players were the most gregarious group in the dorm. I could see how it would be fun, as my father had foretold, to join a fraternity and gain a larger circle of friends, friends to last a lifetime. I did not get to know guys from my classes any more than girls. Classes were not an active area of involvement for me.

All too quickly, after trying the punch known as "Blue Meany" enough to puke on myself and pass out for my only drinking binge, after attending several dances where I listened to mediocre live music while those around me drank themselves into loose appreciation of each others' movements, after wrestling a promising freshman season with ten wins and two losses, after going to most of my physics lectures because they had interesting demonstrations and few of my philosophy lectures because I had never done and never would do the reading, after buying a pair of bell bottoms and wearing them once very self-consciously before relegating them to the floor at the back of my closet, after two terms at the proud school of my destiny, I was deservedly expelled for acquiring consistently abysmal grades. I was given a hearing, a pointless hearing since there was no error in the expulsion. The dean pleased me by mentioning that I was capable of doing the work and shocked me by suggesting that I develop some discipline by doing a tour in the Army.

Out of school! I thought it impossible. I was born with a college diploma, was I not? That is who I was! I should never have to pay such a price for my shortcomings. I had failed to achieve some of my aspirations due to my laziness, but my inborn talents had always been enough, those and the advantages of my white, suburban background. It was almost amusing that I was surprised. It was true that I could not see any way I would have the grades to stay in school. I had handed in a blank paper for my philosophy exam. How did everybody else know how to solve those problems? They must have gone to the classes, taken notes, done the homework.

My mother was more surprised than me. She had
been told all term (by me) that everything was going well.
She wanted to sue the school for not keeping her better
informed. Or for kicking me out when I was clearly able to
continue. At least I was adult enough to talk her out of that.
Dad was more circumspect. He was thinking about what I
should do next. The past was done for him.

VI: Post-college

They packed my stuff into the station wagon and
drove back home quietly, to a home I thought would only
be for my visits, no longer for me to live in. At home I put
my clothes in the laundry hamper. My mother would wash
them although I had learned how to do it myself.

The summer was coming. It would feel completely
normal to do nothing for the summer, but I had to face the
question of what was coming. No longer was the future
determined. My parents talked about my applying to
another school, presumably one with substantially lower
standards. I doubted that was a solution but did not resist. I
knew the problem with my performance was not the
university's high standards. I had not given my classes a
chance. A rumor I had heard, and which turned out to be
true, was that no school would let me in for the year
immediately after my academic suspension. They all
seemed to know that people in my circumstance were a bad
investment. We needed a year of maturity or a year of
facing the facts. I wondered myself if either of those would
help.

By mid-summer, the lingering question in front of
me was "what now?' and the answer that imposed itself was

"get drafted." It was time to confront the draft as more than a social phenomenon.

I was not the only person asking the question although I did not know many as close as me to it. Most of my friends from high school were gone. They were in college, not spending the summer in our home town, and they were holding deferments for the foreseeable future. I knew just a few guys actually in town and made some effort to bring up the subject with them. One guy was trying to eat his way into a medical deferment based on obesity. I wished him luck but did not give that a try. A few other medical deferment ploys were discussed. I had enough ethics (I liked to think it was ethics) in me to refuse to consider harming my body specifically for the deferment. We talked about claiming to be homosexual. I did not see that claim as quite as severe an ethical breach but I had no idea how to make such a claim convincing. It would have taken far more guts than I had to directly refuse the draft and go to jail. I did see that, however, as the most honest option.

Escape to Canada was harder to do. Canada was not a difficult place, I assumed, but leaving my family and the privileges of my birth would be disastrously disorienting. I had not yet reached the point where I wanted to believe I should reject everything that came before me.

I heard stories about guys who "went underground," who lived in America unofficially. Although I had very little official footprint, it was hard to imagine how to live without any at all. I could see getting along without a passport, or even a social security card, but not even a driver's license? Or was there some clever way to get one, as in a spy movie?

Then there was the passive option of waiting it out. Normally I liked the passive option; it was my signature move in school. I had taken ancient history and American history in high school but really did not know much about how long a war takes. I knew the Civil War lasted about four years, a fact that stuck inexplicably in my head, demonstrating I had a brain. I even knew it started in 1860 and ended in 1864. Furthermore, I knew it was America's most deadly war so it had to be counted as a major one for our country. The two world wars began without U.S. participation so I was hazier on their starting dates. Since the length of the war seemed to be affecting me, I looked in the encyclopedia for the spans of the world wars. World War I ran four years from late 1914 and American involvement in World War II ran from 1941 to 1945, again four years.

The encyclopedia did not say when the Vietnam War started. The written account seemed to show it was left over from World War II. U.S. military equipment and advisors were there in 1950. U.S. soldiers were killed in combat there in 1961. But everyone was arguing about whether we were fighting or just advising. Over a hundred Americans were killed in 1962. Was that enough to say we were in a war? Should the war have run its course by the end of four more years, say 1966? Was the end overdue by the time I would be drafted in 1968?

The choices were mine to make, not my parents' or any other authority's. I could see that the practice I had at college in making my own choices did not bode well. One night as I lay awake in bed worrying about the future, I sat up suddenly, turned on the light and resolved to try an organizational technique described to us during freshman orientation, and wrote out my strengths and weaknesses and goals. I had not done it when the school recommended it because I figured I knew myself, but now I thought I ought to pay more attention to my betters. To this point, I had been a success at wrestling and playing cards. I had not succeeded at coursework or girls although I regarded both of these as temporary lags. I wrote down "failures: girls and studies." It was a step forward to acknowledge them. It felt so right to do this, I enthusiastically listed other weaknesses: "can't dance" and "don't follow politics." I thought about adding "need to gain muscle" but decided my wrestling showed I was healthy enough; my build was just genetics. The muscles would not have been for wrestling where the added weight would have just raised me to a higher weight class; they were for girls. It would be fruitless to worry about getting more muscular and I needed to make some serious decisions. My little list showed me my immaturity. Maybe that was the point of making a list. I lacked the courage or the knowledge or the imagination to do any of the things I would need to do to escape the draft. I was too young and irresponsible to maintain a deferment. I was old enough and muscular enough and educated enough to be the weapon in a war I had never tried to comprehend.

Up till then, the war was an abstraction to myself and others in my milieu. I felt opposed to it although I had not thought much about it. At this point, however, I began to reflect more thoroughly and, without doing any research, became more certain it was a bad thing. It was time to see about how to be a conscientious objector. Without consulting my parents, I went to the minister at our church. I knew him and he knew me but I had not been very active in my last year of high school and, of course, had not been to church since going off to college. I knew the assistant pastor better. He is the one who worked with the young people and I had been active in the youth group for several years. I went to the head pastor because I thought this was something that required the most power. I made an appointment and met him in his office. I had shaken his hand at the church door after services many times but only spoken seriously to him once before that I could recall. During confirmation training, I had gone to his office and said I had trouble taking things on faith. He said Jesus was a window into Christianity, that the literal details of ancient documents was not the point and somehow he reassured me with his respectful and poetic conversation.

Now he listened to my description of the situation vis a vis the draft. As I spoke, I wondered how much he had experienced that was relevant to my questions. It occurred to me that he and his assistant were ineligible for the draft, presumably because the church was against war or, at least, against the role of a soldier in war. I was sure he would have been encouraging me to stay out of it but I felt nothing of that sort from him.

I did not go into detail about why I lost my student deferment. He did not care about that anyway. He asked very few questions of me before pronouncing his verdict. According to him, I would not be able to get CO status unless I were a seminary student or otherwise committed to joining the clergy. This seemed unfair to me; not that I could not qualify, and that association with a formal religion would be essential to gaining the status. I had the feeling, for no obvious reason, that he suspected I was objecting to the war just because I was facing the draft. That would have been more rational than the truth. I was not terribly afraid of war, more afraid of alienating groovy young women and delaying my college life for a couple years.

Having exhausted my ideas for getting out of the draft, I called up my draft board and was told I should expect to receive a draft notice before the winter. I told my parents at dinner that night. My mother uncharacteristically said hardly anything. My father said I should volunteer to be an officer which would require a three-year committment. My mother agreed, saying I would otherwise be "cannon fodder." My father's opinion counted for something in this-- he had been an officer in World War II-- but I was growing up that summer and starting to have an independent opinion. I was not going to sign up for an extra year, no matter how much better being an officer would be. Enlisted men could serve as little as two years. That was a very long time in my experience.

With my newly achieved maturity, I took myself to the recruiting station and signed up for the minimum in both time and tank. Flunking out of school placed me where I deserved to be, not as punishment, flunking out is not an ethical issue, not really, not an ethical breech large enough to deserve such a punishment, but it was a reflection of the tier of humanity I has chosen for myself by my behavior.

VII: Training

A week later, I told my parents at dinner that I had received a date for my induction. Dad had two bits of advice: never volunteer and don't be chickenshit. The latter was a term I did not understand at the time and I did not ask him for clarification because it was obvious I was supposed to know it. I later understood that he meant not to be petty. It was more important advice for officers than for grunts[1].

My mother drove me to Hartford to be sworn in. It was a ninety-minute ride, a very long trip. I thought there should have been a closer place to get it all started. The machinery of the draft reached into every town of the country. Why could it not have enough processing centers to permit more convenient kick-offs? I had a paper bag with all the items my notice had suggested, mainly personal things like underwear and toothbrush. The notice had given equal emphasis to listing what ought not to be brought with us, mainly drugs, pornography and knives.

My mother acted as if it were all routine when we departed. She ignored talking about where we were going or why we were going there until Hartford came into view. Then she said without introduction or apparent emphasis "This damn war."

I answered something minimal, maybe just a slurred "yes." She continued, "We never should have gotten into it." She had always been a supporter of the war, not the Democratic Presidents, but Nixon was in then and she supported him. I did not want to argue with her but I was very surprised.

"I thought you supported the war."

"Not now. Not since they took my son."

I remember the words exactly. She spoke in the past tense. I did not think of myself as spent and did not

---

[1]Infantryman of low rank. All Army enlisted men received training as small arms infantrymen; also called Eleven Bravo, referring to the designation of that military occupational specialty (MOS). Sometimes, "eleven bang-bang."

think there was much chance of my failing to return. She was being dramatic but I knew it was a heartfelt drama and not just put on for the occasion. It seemed her support for the war was very shallow, but it would have been stupid to say anything more about it. I said something like "yes" again.

She found the address from the postcard that announced the time and date for me to report. She went around the block looking for a parking space and then double parked in front of the ugly cinderblock building. I slide across the seat and kissed her. She watched me walk inside and then everything was different, as if I had stepped into a movie.

We had a hasty medical inspection and then lined up to swear an oath, the same oath the President swears at inauguration. Then we went out to buses to go to someplace else, which I realized eventually was Fort Dix, New Jersey. It was a long way to go by bus and passed close to the home I had left that morning.

I chatted with the guy seated next to me when we started out. He had proudly graduated from high school and then worked for a couple years in a garage, doing the less skilled things. He was tired of it and saw no future in it so he signed up for the Army. I wanted to ask if he were aware there was a war going on and that he was volunteering for that but I was afraid he would answer "no." Then we fell into talking about Y.A. Tittle and the New York Giants. The details of football, and professional sports generally, were unfamiliar to me. I watched high school football a few times a year with more enthusiasm than comprehension and went to a few college games at my parents' alma mater where the cheering was for the fine old days they had and the days I would have when it was my turn. My turn had lasted one season during which I learned enough about our league but nothing of the pros. We never watched sports on television. Weekends were for better things. I admired his knowledge of the game and the players. Suddenly I began to care about the Giants and yearned for a game to watch. Like an adult, I introduced myself and shook his hand when there was a lull in the conversation. He was Luther. He seemed a smart fellow despite going no farther than high school. He talked a while about the Knicks. I knew even less about basketball. I could rebound better than most and dribbled and shot the ball worse than most. I did not mind hearing about the current stars of the sport and prospects for the Knicks. He even knew what draft picks they were likely to make but when he got into those details, my eyelids were getting heavy. We laid back and dozed our way through the remaining hours of monotonous interstate highway.

It was a cool evening by the time we arrived at Dix. We got a speech from a young guy who did not even have enough stripes to make him a sergeant although I was not sure what the ranks really were. We dumped our stuff in a pile and went to dinner. After dinner, we were issued bedding and clothes. We walked beside a series of storerooms, holding our arms out while item after item was loaded onto us. We did not try on any of the clothes. We were told there would be a chance to make exchanges later. It was all well made, with labels that described them with adjectives listed backwards, such as "shirt, fatigue, olive drab," which I could see was a system to facilitate taking and filling inventory. It was all olive drab except the black boots, white underwear, and a white sheet. I wondered why I had been told to bring underwear.

We went back to our barracks and picked out bunks, but the day was not over yet. We put on a set of clothes, up to the undershirt, then were more or less

marched off to get our haircuts. A row of silent barbers devoted less than a minute on shearing each of us. It felt odd to have the vibrating clippers caress my skull as if I were already bald. We went from the barber to a row of sinks to wash off the remnant hairs. I looked for Luther to commiserate or say something humorous but I could not recognize him or anyone else. They all looked the same with their stark and homely heads, and their T-shirts, but this was not as big a surprise as I got when I looked into the row of mirrors. I could not find myself in the reflections. It was eerie to know I was among those faces and not to be able to find myself. Part of the eeriness was because everyone else in the row had the same blank look into the mirrors, scanning back and forth to find himself. I did not want to appear the fool so I put one hand on my chest and looked for the image that had made the same move. So that was me. Not a good look.

Early the next morning, we packed up everything again and were escorted into new units. I was marched off (informally or sloppily, depending on interpretation, since neither I nor any of the other trainees knew how to march) to my basic training unit. A small group of drill sergeants in crisp OD and the famous Smoky Bear hats very loudly arranged us into rows and columns. They called out our names to get us in the right places and then they huddled among themselves to go over the lists on their clipboards. They happened to be near me so I could hear what they were doing. They were figuring out who had the most education. This worried me. I did not want to be noticed as a drop-out; I was planning to masquerade as a college graduate as much as possible.

I had expected to be drafted as soon as I graduated anyway. I did not remember often that the war and the draft might have ended by then. Maybe that would have helped me focus on the books, but I typically thought of the war as sadly eternal despite my research. It had always been there as far as I noticed. I knew that America's part in the Vietnam War began a finite number of years before I became aware of it, probably at a low level when I was in elementary school, but by the time I was old enough to be conscious of the world beyond my hometown, there was a full war underway. I knew also that it would end someday but it had not moved in that direction as far as I could see; it only got worse every year, unless that was just the effect of reaching an age when I was touched more by world news and my approaching age of draft eligibility.

VIII: Oscar

Soon they settled on a certain Oscar, who was small and blond and bright, and had a PhD in physics and they called out his name and made him the "field first," i.e., the company leader among us trainees. Then they called out other names and made those people the platoon leaders and squad leaders. To my great surprise, I had the sixth most education in the company so I became a trainee squad

leader. Apparently college graduates were not common in
the Army recruits at that time. At the end of basic, most of
the college grads went off to OCS[2] and I was thereafter the
most educated, or nearly so, in all the units I was in, except
for officers, of course, but they did not matter in my day-to-
day existence and I never knew any of them personally.

I did respect our diminutive field first. It was
surprising how easily he fell into his role as our leader,
shouting our marching orders as if he had done all this for
years. I talked to him during chow that night. He did not
want to talk about himself but I squeezed a few facts out of
him. We lingered at the table, talking softly. No else cared
to listen in although we were not saying anything secret
anyway. He was working at a Federal research facility when
he was drafted. He clarified that he held an entry-level
position and had been there less than a year. He said it
comes down to where you are registered. He came from a
place where everyone went to college and had a deferment
so his draft board grabbed anyone they could. This
arrangement did not sound fair, although I had not expected
much fairness anyway. It was not fair that he was drafted, I
thought, that is, it was not fair that the draft board took more
people in some places than others. I might have been dimly
aware that the effect leading to his capture tended to disfavor
those in relatively rich neighborhoods and thus tended to
disfavor me. Despite the importance of the draft system to
my own life and welfare, I had not looked into it much. I
just knew I was opposed to the draft and that I could not
avoid it.

---

[2] Officer Candidate School

The next day a new set of leaders was announced at the morning formation. I was promoted to platoon leader. We had a new field first. The criterion for the new selection was simple and immediately obvious to us. We stood in line by height. The tallest was given the highest position and so on until all the leadership posts were filled. We stayed with these positions through the rest of basic. I have no idea why leadership slots were allocated two different ways or why they decided to make a change after one day. Doing it by education made more sense to me. I supposed they decided to give authority to the most intimidating and height was a measurable proxy for that, but it would have been a poor proxy.

The odder part of this story is how it affected my erstwhile friend, the physicist. Although he made no apparent objection to his demotion, from that second day forward, he never directly obeyed an order again. When the drill sergeant or the field first said "right face," he turned to the left. When the command was "forward march," he would walk in reverse. The drill sergeant yelled at him mightily for a day, saying he was clearly trying to get himself kicked out but that it was also clear he was competent, just... and here a long list of obscene adjectival insults was provided. I thought he was crazy in some way although I lacked specific clinical terminology to describe his condition. At the least, it seemed proper to send him to an officer for a decision. But what they did, after ranting for a few days, was to simply direct him physically. When he went left, they grabbed him by the arm and moved him to the right. He would then continue in the proper direction. And here I saw much more protest and less absurdity in his actions. He would, if given a physical push, go in the right direction, move at the right speed, sit down in class, go to chow, or whatever else we were supposed to do except that they would not give him any weapon. At the range, he was positioned like the rest of us, just not armed, and he would mime the actions we were making. He did not speak to anyone for the remainder of basic. I tried to talk to him, to be sympathetic, to be clandestine if that what he needed, but he never acknowledged that he had ever met me or that I existed as anything more than an object to avoid when walking. The rumor we heard at the end of basic was that he was sent back to his old job in the lab but at the pay of a private. I doubted this rumor because there was no way for us to know where he went.

IX: Harvey

If Oscar suffered the most by the arbitrary assignment of responsibilities, Harvey enjoyed it the most. He was an inch shorter than me, an insignificant amount he would say, and became a platoon leader like me. We were then roommates. In basic, the leaders were assigned two to a room while those less blessed in height were eight to a room. For this reason, I got to know Harvey better than anyone else in the company. I enjoyed him; his bluster was unfamiliar to me since the suburban folks I knew had been taught some amount of reserve. I believed less than half of what he told me, but I felt honored to hear it all, to be given this show he put out. And he treated me as his partner, being roommates. I saw he expected me to back his play although I thought we were all supposed to do that for each other. I did not think of struggles within the unit. He said he was lucky to get in the Army since he had been in prison, although I think he only meant a night in jail. He was the only person I met in basic who thought being there was a form of good luck. He said he had a metal plate in his head from an injury in a street fight. He showed me the place but I saw nothing noteworthy, just his nearly bald scalp; no scar visible in my casual glance. The sound it made when he rapped it demonstratively was not unlike the sound any of our heads would make although I am sure it sounded different to Harvey. Though he was so different from anyone I had ever known, he was not very different from some TV representations of an urban drop-out. Nonetheless, he contrasted with my expectation that blacks would be socially conscious and liberal. Harvey was politically conservative, supportive of the war, and actively hated hippies. I could honestly say I was no hippy and I did not tell him I wished I had the guts and the cool to be one.

Harvey was as abusive to his platoon as the limited powers of our leadership allowed. He wanted no friends, other than me, who was his back-up. One night as we were lying in bed, he told me of a fight he claimed to have had in a bar, a fight where his drunken opponent tried to wrestle him to the ground. As Harvey told the tale he had stayed away from the drunk and darted in to punch until his attacker was unconscious. I interpreted his story as a claim that my alleged skills in wrestling would not compare with his alleged skills in boxing. I did not express a position on him relative to me but I did want to defend my sport. Nonetheless, I did have a position on him relative to me. I thought I was a good wrestler, trained and tested, but he was untrained, a big talker and not even especially physically fit, just moderately big and aggressive. I figured even a good boxer would only get one good blow in before a good wrestler got a grip and then the wrestler would win.

I defended my sport and he got very excited. He sat up and said we should test out our theories. We would have a fight on the next day. I did not see that a contest between us would clarify whether wrestling or boxing was superior although I did not say I suspected I could beat him in any contest.

After breakfast we had time to clean up the barracks. Harvey announced we were going to have a fight. I objected, of course. I had meant for a private contest of techniques, not a public exhibition and not a "fight." But my words were too subtle for the situation. Within minutes, there were fifty or sixty trainees around us in the common room of our barracks.

Harvey made little stretching motions as if he knew how to warm up. He punched the air in short combinations. I figured it would not last long and no one would get hurt so I said "Okay, let's do it." It went just as I expected. I went low, approaching him with one hand on the floor. He never even took a swing before I had his heel and took him to the ground. I pinned him immediately. He whined "Get the hell off me," and I let him up. I told everyone to get back to cleaning the barracks and tried to calm Harvey down, saying it was just a sporting contest.

Harvey was livid. He screamed that it was no game; that I had not beaten him, just managed to sit on him; that he would kill me. I explained that being able to pin him proved I could control him. A pin was better than a beating. Then he reached into an unused locker and took out a metal tent stake. He swiped it at me as if it were a knife. I thought it was funny that when I dodged his swipe, he backed off as if I had a knife. He was putting on a show that he believed was real. I appealed to the crowd around us to grab him and disarm him, but not a soul wanted this to end so easily. I feinted and then grabbed Harvey's wrist, twisted it, and threw him to the floor. It was a standard move we practiced in wrestling but which we never used in matches because it was too obvious. I pinned him again since that is what I was trained to do. I spoke to him, pointing out that I controlled him readily. He scratched at my face with his free hand. It was something respectable males would never do in my world. I wrapped an arm around his throat and blocked off the blood flow to his brain. It was a move we had been shown because it was illegal and had to be avoided, but I had tried it a few times outside the gym and knew it would knock him out within a few seconds. He went limp and I stood up. I brushed myself off dramatically before taking the stake from his limp hand. I reassured everyone that he would be fine.

Harvey convulsed a little as he regained consciousness. He did not attack me again but he threatened me in every way he could. He said he would kill me in bed and I should never go to sleep while he was around. I did not believe him although I was just smart enough to know I could not be certain. In the morning formation the drill sergeant asked what happened to my face. The scratches could not be explained as anything but what they were. I said we had worked it out. He wanted to know who I had fought but he did not try too hard. He said he would take it up again that night. Harvey disappeared during lunch, went "over the wall," that is AWOL. I never heard of him again. I doubted he would have been a good soldier; it is not a profession for a big ego.

After the wrestling-boxing contest, I was viewed with respect by the guys in the immediate unit although I did not notice it much or maybe I just did not want to be aware of it. Maybe I just assumed it was natural. I did not think the contest was noteworthy; it had not been much of a contest. And then a small delegation came to me to say they had arranged a race between me and a guy in a nearby company. I did not mind a race until they mentioned it would be a sprint. And it was just between me and their guy. And there was already heavy betting on it. I was no sprinter. Apparently their guy was. I was angry that they had not asked me about the race before committing me to it. I would have been better in a longer race. I might have bet on myself at a distance over a mile. I was no miler, but no one here was likely to beat me. In a sprint, I would have been mediocre. Sprints are for the muscular ones. I gave it little thought and refused to run. I said I would not win. It occurred to me to offer some other excuse, say that I did not gamble, but I knew the most persuasive argument would be to admit I would lose. There was a possibility of winning, I thought. Their guy might have been caught up in his own bluster. I was not going to risk that. It was better to lose my immortality than to lose their money.

I told them I was quick, not fast. At the morning formation, someone called out "skinny-quick," and that's who I had become. I never said I was a sprinter, never saw my challenger, and never ran the race, but I could not object to the name. They had to respect my wrestling or beat me at it, and no one wanted to risk losing to my less-than-commanding physique. Everyone was satisfied with calling me "skinny" and calling me "quick." The drill sergeant would call me "Quick," but that was just because he called everyone by his last name.

X: Tests

Early in boot camp, we took a series of standardized tests, like the SATs. I liked these tests when I was in school and I liked them in the Army because I did well on them, better than on the tests in class. They are the reason I was viewed in school as an underachiever, a far better circumstance, in my view, than being incapable even if all authorities said otherwise. My mother had understood standardized tests would be my ticket to university so she hired a tutor for me and signed me up for practice tests to improve my scores. I was not in the top one percent, but I was usually close enough to the top percentile that I could believe I belonged there, given the errors in testing.

Up to this point, the Army had me buried in the mass of mediocrity of enlisted recruits, but the tests, I expected, would set me apart. I would be separated, offered opportunities, respected. This seemed all the more likely when I observed my fellow test takers who showed no interest in performing well. This was not a group trying to get into the best college they could; the room was a bizarre parody of the gymnasium where I took the SAT.

The first test was an easy version of the verbal SAT. The next test was less reassuring. It covered mechanical skills, such as car and lawn mower repair, very weak points in my background. I wanted to feel cheated by this subject matter but I could see it was fair. So I accepted I would have some middling scores in areas of less importance. Then we had one on "general knowledge." Even the questions outside my experience on this test were going my way-- I knew the answer to how do you reduce the head on a beer (pour along the side of the glass or put in a little salt), even though I hated to drink beer, so I regained some confidence.

Then we had a test which was described in the introductory notes as "psychological," and therefore, as having no right answers. I did not believe there were no right answers. Maybe there were not answers that could be compared to verifiable facts, but there had to be more or less favorable outcomes that might follow from the answers given. I thought I had an edge on the others because I had taken psychology in my good university and had paid attention to some of the lessons on designing tests. So I surmised that some questions were used because their answers corresponded well with characteristics the test designers want to identify, even if the designers did not know why those answers were so revealing. And I also knew it was a common ploy in such tests to repeat a question of particular importance. So I played against the designers to make my score demonstrate my desirability to the Army for, for-- I was not sure what.

In the end the test was frustrating because I could not see the point of it. And yet I still recall the two questions that were repeated on the test and my answers. One was "Do you like to handle guns?" This sounded perverse to me. I thought the test was looking for people who had come to the Army for the wrong reasons, because they want to shoot people rather than want to defend freedom. By the time I finished my Army experience, I knew my interpretation of this question was wrong. The Army preferred a "yes" on this one.

The other repeated question was "Which do you prefer: sand or lightning?" The best interpretation I could devise was that sand represented the day-to-day experience of the infantry while the lightning represented the action of combat. I assumed combat would be a rare thing in the life of most GIs, even during the Vietnam War. So this was searching for those who would be willing to put up with the drudgery of infantry rather than seeking the rare thrills. Subsequent experience confirmed the rarity of time in combat but nothing ever helped me understand what this question was measuring. I handled it correctly, I think. I was so uncertain about its purpose, I answered "sand" once and "lightning" once. During the test, I gave a quick thought to the actual answer to this question, i.e., to which I preferred. I did not mind either and did not feel any affinity for either. Maybe that helped me toward my ambiguous responses.

Boot camp is famous for its supposed physical rigors. Its actual requirements could not be terribly hard since we effectively were limited by the abilities of the weakest among us. The classroom time was even farther from expectations, from the classrooms that dominated my responsibilities since I was six. The teachers generally had memorized every word of our lessons. They recited lectures like terrible poetry. If I listened closely, they would make sense, but, of course, I rarely listened closely. As far as I could tell, no one listened closely. In every class, someone was assigned to keep everyone else awake. The person on this duty would walk around the classroom and tap the head of anyone dozing off. Anyone who felt sleepy was supposed to stand in the back of the room. This was based on the supposition that we could not sleep while standing. By the end of basic, I knew this was a bad assumption. We were so sleep-deprived, we regularly slept while standing in formation. Since the officers did not acknowledge this as sleep, it was more acceptable than sleeping on the ground while waiting for whatever was next. Waiting was our most common activity.

The classes covered a wide range of topics, ranging from those I already knew to those I did not want to know. For example, they were very serious about teaching us how to take care of our feet. I certainly was not going to admit to myself that I did not know how to take care of my feet already. I must have known how to do it since I never had any problem with them. However, a little did sink in. I heard their point, and accepted it, that circumstances in the field might go outside the range of my experience to date, that we might be in a situation where we were unable to change our clothes every morning. The name "trenchfoot" had a military association and a disgusting implication after we saw pictures of it. The two hour-long classes on this subject might have done me some good; my take-away was to try to get dry socks on every day.

I was even more humbled by the lesson on brushing teeth. When I saw the topic for the class written on the board at the door of the classroom, I knew the class had nothing for me but that it might be good for some of the people with impoverished backgrounds. You had to be pretty backward to need lessons on brushing teeth at our age. They talked in detail about how to brush your teeth, all very familiar stuff. Then they gave us a tablet to chew. It stained the food proteins on our teeth. We were given tooth brushes and toothpaste and told to brush off the dye. They claimed the dye adhered only to the food particles and that removing it was equivalent to removing the food. I brushed my teeth and then looked in the mirror. Not only was I shocked by the quantity of dye remaining, I was shocked at how bad I looked with red dye all over my teeth. I had to get it off or I would be the hillbilly. I doubted the dye was only on food particles so I scrubbed one portion as a test. And it got white. So I scrubbed the rest of my teeth desperately, before anyone noticed my poor hygiene. I had to admit I learned something that day, but, until now, I only admitted it to myself.

We had a class in "command voice" that seemed entirely inappropriate for me. I did not expect to be giving any commands. The lesson was silly (how to speak with a sound of authority) and seemed to be directed at future officers, who probably had plenty of silly classes. I understood some voices were more authoritative than others and I would have liked to have a better voice, but one's voice came from genetics, or so I believed. I may have learned a tiny bit in this class and may have used it a tiny bit in my military and subsequent career, but I certainly learned to recognize people who were projecting their voice to be more authoritative. It was a common sound and style to hear from the throats of officers. I always laughed at them for having relearned how to talk, even in civilian applications.

There were, obviously, classes in weaponry, lots of deadly hardware, just as anyone would expect. And key among all of these was the rifle: securing it, disemsembling it, cleaning it, carrying it, parading it, firing it. In basic, everyone is an infantryman. They told us everyone in the Army will always be an infantryman as either a first or second military occupational specialty. The fascination with the rifle went beyond its utility as an instrument of war; it was a symbol of the supremacy behind the military which provided the weapon. We were to absorb the rifle until we gained the confidence that its power brought to us more personal power than we had known as civilians. It was odd to me that this cult of the infantry would be promoted because it seemed to me (although I admit I was poorly informed) infantry was the worst specialization one could have in the Army and I, for one, would have preferred any of the many other options even though I could see, and was right to see, that I was headed without delay or detour into the infantry.

This is my rifle. (*raise your rifle*)
This is my gun. (*grab your crotch*)
This is for fighting. (*point to your rifle*)
This is for fun. (*point to your crotch*) (How juvenile!)

XI: First Actual Duty

Towards the end of basic, we were called out of our planned training for a special assignment. The outside world had impinged upon us. We were told we would be guarding the camp perimeter, guarding it for real, not from Vietnamese, of course, but from American protesters. We

were not told the nature of the protest, but the implication
was that they might try to break into Fort Dix. I could not
see how breaking into the fort grounds would accomplish
anything, but I often did not understand why protests took
the form they did. Probably it was a good idea if it induced
media coverage.

I was excited to think a demonstration might reach
to us although I felt I was on the wrong side of it. How
embarrassing to be the young, skinny, bald private standing
guard against the long-haired, ethical, groovy protesters!
And yet I did not consider protesting along with them. On
one hand, I did not know exactly what they were protesting
and had no way to contact them to learn more about it, but
much more than that, more realistically, when the idea arose
of joining them in any way, I was scared by it. I would be
taking a far greater risk than any of them because I would be
breaking "direct orders." I would be in the brig facing court
martial. I envisioned any risk they faced as being at most a
night of singing songs in a local jail, while I would be in a
lonely place indefinitely with a ruined future. Despite the
social disreputability of being a soldier during the Vietnam
War, I still fully expected to get out of the Army in two years
and back into college where I would do better than before
(my confidence in my fate was too important to abandon
although some subconscious doubt must have been
germinating), where I would not mention my history of the
previous few years, and where I would be forever insulated
from being drafted.

We were sent to a building on a part of the base we
had not seen before. Each platoon was given a room in the
austere concrete structure. When we arrived, there was
nothing in our room but air. We sat or stood about for

thirty minutes, not a long wait by our standards, until an officer came to explain the situation, that is, as much of the situation as was appropriate for us to know. We would be issued M-16s[3] but no ammunition. He reminded us, as we had often been reminded, that anyone having a round of live ammunition in his possession at any time off the range was subject to arrest and court martial. Nonetheless, our platoon constituted a formidable gang capable of and, likely, willing to commit more violence than I had ever seen first-hand.

He did not say we would be issued ammunition if the circumstances demanded it. I wondered what good a rifle would be without ammunition. It was explained to us that the main reason we were not being issued ammunition was because the Army did not trust us yet, that we were not trained yet. I just barely understood that he was referring to training in discipline rather than training in technical use of the weapon. As an aside, he said the rifle is a substantial weapon even when not loaded. This I did not believe although I later realized, when better trained and experienced in carrying the M-16 around with me, that I was wrong about that.

He did not say, but we all thought, the real purpose of giving us M-16s was to make us look threatening. We would not be proud of looking dangerous under false pretenses, although most of us would have been happy to project a dangerous outlook back in the world, i.e., in civilian existence. But soon we were about to be actually dangerous, more dangerous than most of us, certainly more than I, could imagine. It was an insult to merely pretend to

---

[3] The rifle used by U.S. troops.

be capable of deadly force, carrying an empty weapon. We had fired live rounds into targets for some weeks and walked short courses through the field with human-shaped pop-ups that we shot through; and tried out .45s[4], M-50s[5], grenade launchers and hand grenades; and set up and fired off live mines.

After the officer left, we waited for several hours. It was a cold day and our empty room had a hard, cold concrete floor. We sat on our rolled up rain ponchos or leaned against the wall. We smoked cigarettes. Our physical discomfort was not important although we were all aware of it; every day was uncomfortable.

The talk in the room amazed me for it centered on whether we would fire on Americans if ordered to do so. I was surprised by the question since we had been told we would not be given ammunition. I was also surprised that people were addressing an essentially political question. And I was pleased and surprised that everyone who spoke about this said he would not. On this question, I was not sure about myself and I did not boast of my courage to defy orders. It was not critical to me that the protesters were Americans. If we were going to fire on people when ordered to do so, I would not expect to judge whether those people deserved it. That oath we took so solemnly back in Hartford disturbingly included the phrase "all enemies, foreign and domestic."

Eventually the time for chow came around and we were marched off to the mess hall. We had not been issued M-16s and we never heard if there had been a protest or,

---

[4] The standard pistol carried by officers.
[5] Machine guns

obviously, what form it took. It had been a day that left us with sore rumps, and although it was unique, it still managed to be boring. We had missed out on training but I had learned as much as on any day and what I learned was mostly about myself and it did not make me proud.

XII: Knife

Conducting war is in some ways the ultimate masculine enterprise. Pure make-believe is the childish start of it and sports is just a further boyish imitation. Competition for whatever pleasures there might be in human existence tends to drive us, at least in the culture I have experienced, and war is its supreme expression. And yet in practice, for those of us at the level of cannon fodder, preparation for war is entirely dependent on our immaturity making us vulnerable to bullying, peer pressure and insecure egos. The actual implementation of war, as this tale will tell, relies on yet another factor, not obvious during the training phase-- the child's will to win regardless of the game.

I was slightly aware how the training system was manipulating us and laughed silently at the faux anger of our drill sergeants, yet granting them some leeway in recognition of their task to bring to heel our diverse, unruly, and broadly incompetent lot. But my insight into their task fell short of lifting me to mature behavior at many critical moments. And why should it? The situation called for maturity, for careful responses, but so had entering college been an appropriate time to put aside shortsighted, self-indulgent decisions and I had made no progress in that direction. I did not know it yet, but I was a very slow learner despite increasingly powerful incentives. Yet, I did learn something eventually and I was extremely fortunate to have the time for some of the critical lessons before I was jailed or injured. Not everyone had this simple good luck.

Before AIT[6], I took two weeks of leadership training, having been selected out of basic training for my potential as an infantryman. My leadership school and AIT were in barren and dreary Ft. Polk, Louisiana in the summer of 1968, one year after the "summer of love," and here I came into my own within the modest milieu of Army trainees. The early hours; the constant exercise; the acceptance of rank; the discomfort of weather; the boredom of simple, rote lectures; and myriad other artifices of the military required no effort on my part; I welcomed their stress-free demands. They were so much easier than making small talk at a fraternity mixer with girls, attractive or not; or taking notes in biochemistry where I was expected to know everything that was said and to relate it to the textbook that I had to read on my own time; or finding clothes that were stylish enough to speak well of me without being absurd in an era when style was changing rapidly in ways I did not comprehend. Army training was oddly less serious than my familiar stresses and pursuits, and I felt good at it. I was not inclined, like most of the people around me, to complain about it all. I did not like it, but it was relaxing to have so little responsibility. I did not think deeply enough to appreciate the irony of how serious it was or how much responsibility I would carry when they gave me a loaded rifle and sent me to a combat zone.

Life was working as I now thought it ought to be, coasting along with my temporary rank among trainees, the

---

[6] Advanced infantry training.

respect of the drill sergeants, and the occasional ego gratification from scoring well on the PT[7] test. I was the athlete and genius I was supposed to be. But toward the end of the first week of AIT, I sensed resentment from one of the guys in my platoon. Franklin, the last name above his breast pocket, was short, uneducated, and black, hardly the characteristics I expected to be worthy of challenging me. But he was reluctant to accept my orders although my orders were never arbitrary, only the necessary to move the unit from formation to chow or firing range. I did not enjoy the power of my little rank, only the respect of it. And then one day when we happened to be sitting near each other and no one else, waiting for the next thing, he muttered something about my being a phony. I said something back, not something aggressive, something like "No phony; just a trainee like you." He did not accept that point. I had privileges and I was no better than him. Of course he was right except that it was hardly news that the Army was arbitrary or that people like me were likely to be favored by America's institutions over people like him.

"What can you do?" he asked me. I looked at him more closely. He had a handsome face; very dark skin; thick muscles. I had talents to show him, tricks I did to impress people or win a bet in a bar. I ran through my repertoire mentally. I could pick up a dollar at my feet when standing with my heels against a wall without bending my knees. I never knew anyone else who could do that one, but we did not have a wall nearby and it was not the sort of thing to satisfy him. Without a word, I went over to a tree, placed my hands a certain way on the trunk and lifted myself

---

[7] Physical training.

into a horizontal position, carrying my weight mostly on one elbow propped into my hip. He watched me silently and when I lowered myself back down, he went to the tree and held it with his hands and lifted himself horizontal like a flag. His body did not form a T with the tree as mine had, his entire weight was on one side of the tree. I did not know it was possible to do this. It would only be possible for a very stocky and very strong person. "Nize," I said, quoting Mr. Natural.[8] "I wrestle. Put me in any hold you want." I hoped he was not a wrestler because, if he were, I did not know where this might go. I had in mind I would resign my rank. He stood beside me and I saw anew how much shorter he was than me. He was very stocky but still significantly lighter than me, I supposed. He moved behind me and put on a full nelson. I fought off a smile. This was not a good hold, not a hold any wrestler would use, and not a good hold for his short arms and low angle. I bent my knees to make it easier for him. "Are you set?" I asked. He said he was and I slipped to the ground, twisting to grab his ankle and rolled on top of him. With my weight on his chest and my arms wrapped to keep him from turning over, he did not struggle further.

"So you can wrestle."

"Yeah."

That night he came into my room. As the platoon leader, I had a private room at the end of barracks He offered to shine my boots for the morning inspection. I refused, of course, but he insisted he did not mind. He was, and we both knew it, much better at shining boots than I

---

[8] A character in an early underground comic, likely known only by urban, liberal-minded youth.

was. He said he wanted his unit to look the best and I was letting it down. Suddenly I saw him as a potential career soldier, not a screw-up like me who was caught in the draft. He had a better claim to being platoon leader; maybe he actually thought we were doing something meaningful. I said I could use instruction from him, that he could come into my room to teach me the trick of getting a good shine, and that is what he did every night for the rest of AIT.

What I remember about that room is the hole in the plaster. Having the room made me a little uncomfortable; I preferred to feel the same hardships as everyone else. I craved the respect of my peers, and getting it from my superiors was less than helpful. The hole was memorable for how I used it.

We were constantly being given instruction during those months of basic training and AIT, treated like idiots, as by as an overly indulgent mother except that most of these guys did not have overly indulgent mothers. ...But I did and I resented their nagging more than hers since I had no compulsion to love the Army. However, most of their nagging was needed by someone among us. I interpreted most of it as applying to them rather than to me; I already knew, even if I was not consistent in applying the knowledge, the importance of brushing my teeth, washing my socks and underwear, sitting up straight, eating fruits and vegetables, and pointing my rifle only down-range.

It was not surprising that I would ignore very good instruction from my superiors; I had always managed to project the impression of being well behaved while actually doing about as I wanted. I did not think of myself as arrogant or rebellious, although the rebellious times were seeping into my persona; it being such a fine justification for my failures to believe the system around me was corrupt in ways that disfavored the inherently good, like myself.

On the day we practiced using bayonets for the first time, I was especially haughty. There was nothing unobvious in our lesson. We placed the bayonets on our rifles, fitting onto a simple attachment mechanism. Then we waited our turn to charge ten yards to a straw target. We stabbed it any way that seemed convenient; the instructors were entirely focused on the charge. They insisted it be vigorous, which was measured by the volume of the scream you made when it was your turn. It was embarrassing to be playing at soldier when we were soon to be real soldiers. Even when I was ten, at my peak appreciation of World War II, I would not have found any thrill in the game of standing in line, bored and sweaty, for my time to run screaming across parched grass to a scarecrow target with a nearby adult begging me to make it realistic by showing my (faked) emotions.

It was one of those days when the training lacked any practical value, as if someone had said we must have bayonet training but no one knew what to teach. I saw their harping on the danger of a bayonet as part of the silliness to make it meaningful; our bayonets were real enough, but dull as toys. After a couple hours of this drill, we all qualified as "experts." This would mean we could add a bar with the word "bayonet" to our expert badge.

We in the small arms infantry trained in and were assessed in many weapons, with our rating in each worn on our dress uniform. It made us look accomplished and dangerous. We would not wear the bayonet bar, however, since anyone who knew anything of it would see it was just another dangle. Getting the expert rating in rifle was worth showing, we thought, but we only wore them once, on the trip back home after AIT. Only recent trainees actually wear their expert badges, except with class-A uniforms that we never wore anyway.

With the exercise finally over, we ceremoniously turned in our bayonets. They were kept in a locked box, not as secure as rifles, but the act of returning them was excessively officious. I espied a flaw in their security system and to prove my courage and cleverness, I secreted a bayonet and a sheath in my pack. Then I marched my platoon onto the trucks for transport back to the barracks and mess.[9]

By the time we were back, there was an officer waiting for us to complain that a bayonet was missing. I was impressed at the efficiency of this development, and a little worried it might cause me some problem. However, I moved my men into formation, giving a certain squad enough ambiguity that a few fellows headed inside to the head. I gave them a minute for their escape and then loudly went after them. I wore my pack throughout these maneuvers and deftly slung it off, extracted the bayonet and dropped it into the hole in my wall. I soon had my whole platoon lined up, settling them into formation before any of the other platoons in the company, so we could endure the officer's rant about weapon security. He offered amnesty for anyone helping to find the bayonet and the brig for anyone caught with it otherwise, but I was not tempted to turn myself in. How could anyone take the officer seriously? He was like an elementary school teacher telling

---

[9] "Mess" is military-speak for meals. It has no connotation about the food quality.

us to put our heads down and not look until the guilty party has put the missing pencil back on his desk. It had all been so simple; no one saw anything suspicious in me; I was good enough. I had spit in the face of the Army and if the Army was pissed about it, so much the better.

And I was right in my assessment except for Franklin. He did not say anything until after mess when we were cleaning up for the night. He was working a push broom across the barracks floor until he reached my office, where I was sitting on the bunk reading an anthology of poetry from the camp library. He came in the room and started to sweep it too so I jumped up and took it from him. "Thanks, Franklin. I'll get this."

While I swept, he stood by the door watching me and when I gave the broom back to him he said, "It was you."

"What?" I answered. It is surely what I would have said if I were entirely innocent although it sounded guilty at that moment. That compact knot of muscle had been studying me for a month. He knew me better than I knew myself. It was not admiration; probably curiosity. I was outside the range of people in his experience just as far as he was outside the range of people I had ever known. I could have convinced myself I did not take the bayonet easier than I could have convinced him. My mind quickly envisioned some kind of blackmail. He had never asked for any favors in return for maintaining my boots. Was he waiting for a chance like this? What would he want that I could give?

He knew and I knew that he knew, but he went ahead and reiterated his point anyway.

"You don't even want it."

With that remark, I relaxed. He might see his future in the Army, but at this stage, it was not doing him any good and he would spit in its face too.

XIII: Sex and Tattoos

If college life had been a fruitless search for a sexual partner underlying all else, underlying Army training was the temporary abandonment of all sexual aspiration. The explicit talk of sex all day long turned the whole subject into a running joke. Maybe there were homosexual contacts somewhere in those camps, but I never saw any hint of them. Maybe the apparent draft deferment for homosexuality was part of that.

The only actual sexual experience I knew of during training took me by surprise. Toward the end of training, we were on a field exercise, an overnight trip in the dry Louisiana pinelands, and we had reached our objective for the time being, a point on a map, so we were waiting for something else to do. It was a common thing during training, waiting for a few hours. We were lying in the shade using our packs as backrests, twenty or so trainees. There was no drill sergeant around. A civilian came walking out of the field before us. No one got up; we just waited for him to come on. It was very odd to see a civilian in the field. We thought of ourselves as being in a remote place, but as we stared at the approaching figure, we could see he had come from a parked car. It was odder still to see a civilian in a place like this dressed in urban clothes. He wore an unbuttoned dress shirt over his t-shirt and pressed pants and black leather shoes. I figured his car had broken down. There would not be anything we could do for him. I was not curious enough to listen to the animated conversation he had with the guys on his end of our line.

Soon a few guys wandered off with him, back to his car. After a while I was bored of leaning on my pack and I stood up to take a drink of water from my canteen. About then, the group of guys came back across the field. The car was gone so I guessed at least one of them had some mechanical knowledge, but I was far off in my guesses.

They came back with a story that there was a prostitute in the car and one of them, the youngest, most innocent looking one, has decided to try her out. He was in the car for only a couple minutes and paid fifty dollars. That was a lot of money to us. I would never have had that much on me. He had not even had real sex with her, no penetration, and had not even been allowed to touch her as he wanted, so he was disappointed about that although he apparently had an ejaculation. The strangest part of his story was that he told it rather than lie to us. I had heard of prostitutes, of course, but never been this close to actually seeing one. I did not figure I had missed much.

It was similar to my first exposure to tattoos, which was an equally obscure and disreputable subject I knew to exist but had never encountered. I doubt I had even seen a tattoo directly but, in contrast with prostitutes, I had seen real ones in pictures. I did not want either one but the prostitute seemed like a choice I was making to not want, while the tattoo was an absurdity. Maybe I was just more scared of the prostitute. No, I was definitely more scared of the prostitute (her expertise, her diseases and her pimp) but I also feared the tattoo (diseased needles). Its only attraction was that my mother sometimes said I was forbidden to have one and that hardly seemed like enough justification to get one.   In my understanding, it was a tradition of Pacific islanders and World War II soldiers.

On our last day in AIT, there was an agitated group slow to get into the breakfast formation. Usually in the morning no one had much to say so I was a little curious. They were examining the upper arm of a quiet, small chested southern fellow and I thought he had some kind of injury or cancer or insect bite. On the night before, he had slipped into town, to the strip of shops and bars next to the base, and gotten a tattoo. I peeked into the crowd and got a glimpse of it, an Army logo placed so it would not show below his T-shirt sleeve-- "U.S. Army." How could he feel so strongly attached to the army when all he had done was endure a few months of training? Not only did he come from somewhere in American culture that I had never seen, he must have been desperate to belong to something. I could see that some people might be proud of being in the Army, once they had done something in it but it did not occur to me that anyone at this point in our history would think merely joining was worth commemorating for life.

XIV: Trophy

With three days left in AIT, I was called out of the morning formation. While everyone else went to breakfast, I went to the Captain's office. It was my first time there. I had never spoken to him and he had never spoken to me as an individual but this day he answered my salute and my "reporting as ordered" with a casual touch of his forehead and a motion toward the chair as if we were friends or, at least, colleagues. He called the First Sergeant to come in and then informed me that I had been selected to represent

the company in the competition for "trainee of the cycle."
The "cycle" referred to all trainees in AIT at this time. I
had never heard of such a competition and wondered what I
had done to be selected like this although, on the other
hand, it did seem right and now that I knew of it, I wanted it.
If someone was needed to represent our company, it should
be me.

The next step in the process would be an interview
at the battalion HQ in the afternoon. He was giving me the
morning off so I could read the newspapers. Knowing
current events, he explained, figured highly in the battalion
assessment. I was not clear on exactly what a battalion was
but I assumed it was one step up from company. I was not
clear on lots of military points. I had not studied anything
since basic began. I did not take notes in class. It was all
too easy to bother with any more mental effort although
there was a dim sense that some part of it might matter if I
ended up in Vietnam. I did put out energy in physical
training and that got me noticed, which was all I really
wanted. It did not require any effort to get the maximum
score on the written tests they gave us, so I looked good to
the Captain, but I was aware that I did not actually know
much about the military, such as what the maximum
effective range was for each of the weapons we covered, or
what were the ranks of other branches of the military.

The first sergeant gave me a local newspaper,
containing no national or international news, and a stack of
magazines, including most productively, a recent issue of
Time, and sent me off to a solitary breakfast. I had little
background on current events before I was drafted although
it was probably as much as any of the trainees, unless there
was an Oscar in the battalion, but Oscar would not have

been selected as a representative because, I assumed illogically, PT would have been the first criterion. The interview at battalion would not include a PT test. I read the magazines while lying on my bunk, a pleasant morning. The platoon came back to the barracks before chow so I joined them for lunch although I did not assume command of them in the lunch formation. No one knew what was going on with me. I did not explain and was not offended that no one asked. It would be a triumph when my morning's activity was announced.

After lunch I sat outside the Captain's office with the pile of magazines in my lap. I had read them and there were no more so I did not do much at all. After a couple hours, the first sergeant came out and announced the call had come through for me to go to battalion. He too was treating me like a colleague which made me feel uncomfortable, disoriented after these months of being kept separate from those in the real Army, lifers. His easy banter on the walk over to battalion relaxed me for the interview. I was normally good in interviews, self-confident and articulate-- as long as I did not get questions about the things I should have learned in our classes. Two Captains and a First Lieutenant conducted my interview. It was all very cordial. I recognized that I had come from an officer's socio-economic background and these people were familiar to me. Mostly they chatted about my background before coming to the Army. I avoided saying I was kicked out of school. In fact, I avoided saying I had not finished college. I was not sure how much was in the records they held on me and saw no reason to bring out my weak points. Mostly I talked about wrestling in college. It was very smooth; no questions about weaponry. Only one vague reference to current events in the form of whether I got along well with the hippies who surely had been at my university. The last question came from the lieutenant. What did I think of the Army Code of Conduct. It seemed an odd question and I said positive things about the way they made us behave, the need for discipline with a diverse population. I told a little story about the range of fellows at my induction ceremony and how effective the military methods had been in bringing them together.

After dinner that night, the CO announced I was the Company Trainee of the Cycle. He gave me a small trophy and everyone clapped. No one mentioned it to me afterwards. I was disappointed that I was not the battalion selection. It did not really surprise me. I did not know who was in the other companies.

A few months later I was issued a card to keep in my wallet. It bore the heading "The Army Code of Conduct." It listed the six articles of the Code, beginning with "I am an American, fighting in the forces which guard my country and our way of life. I am prepared to give my life in their defense." These are the rules for behavior if taken prisoner. Why would that be the only technical question they would ask me? We had covered it very briefly in class, too brief for me to recall. It all made simple sense and was so unlikely to be relevant, I had not tried to memorize it. It was something for officers and pilots. I was neither of those and I was not the battalion trainee of the cycle, and I did not deeply regret any of these three omissions to my biography.

There was one last formation in AIT with the full company, the one where we got our follow-up assignments. I had applied to every school and assignment other than

Vietnam that the company clerk could find: signal corps (I took a test to see how well I could discern the difference in sound between a dot and a dash, and did not score well), translator (entry also based on a test of basic abilities rather than training to date and also far beyond my ability), special services as a wrestler (the Army apparently had sports teams when it had good athletes although my good freshman year was nothing by Army-wide standards), guard at Washington's Tomb of the Unknown Soldier (I was very near meeting the strict height and weight guidelines), sharpshooter, jump school, and others I cannot remember. Lots of guys applied to various things with the same idea of getting out of Vietnam or, at least, out of the infantry. We had even been asked once to fill in a form saying what geographic assignment we would like. I had answered "Alaska" because I doubted many people would say that so I might actually get it.

The First Sergeant read through the roll and said where each of us would go next. Someone was destined to be a cook and three guys with commercial licenses became drivers. Someone else was given an assignment in a word none of us could understand. No one was sent to Alaska. Other than me, the rest of the company heard the same two syllables after their names were called-- it sounded liked "vet-num." I was assigned to jump school in two words, and, in two more syllables, given my next destiny: "vet-num."

XV. Getting Out of Polk

The stolen bayonet came back to me one more time. I extracted it from the wall using a bent clothes hanger

on our last night in AIT. I stashed it deep in my duffle bag.
It would be a souvenir whose origins would remain ever
secret and whose meaning would console me whenever I
thought of the drudgery of Army training. In the morning
we went to a transit site across base to await buses to the city.
We were all really pleased to be putting this part of
Louisiana behind us.

An E-7[10] called us into formation. He had us put
our duffels on the ground and marched us off to the shade.
Then a contingent of troops we did not know started going
through the luggage. The sergeant explained he was
searching for Army contraband, for anything stolen from the
Army and was doing it in full view of all of us so we could be
sure his crew did not themselves steal anything. Here was a
trick I had not seen before. He offered no amnesty and I
wondered if I would have taken it or simply awaited my fate.
The inspectors dumped out one duffle at a time and
scratched through its contents. They left everything in a pile
and went on to the next one. They were about halfway
through when the sergeant announced it was time for chow
and we should repack the duffles they had inspected. He
said he would look at the rest after we ate, but I never saw
him again. Luck had come my way again.

XVI: Transit

After jump school, short trip home to see my
parents and then a week in Ft. Lewis, Washington waiting
for my turn to go... When I woke on the third day at Lewis,
the quiet informed me that the rain had dissipated and the

---

[10] Platoon sergeant.

skies had cleared. I went outside, excited by the change which seemed to move me closer to my big trip overseeas. I had not been informed Mt. Rainier was right there, next to us, but there was it was, looming in a way no photo could have conveyed. For the first time in my Army experience, I felt I was someplace unique. All day I looked to that presence and wondered how I could not have known it was there through those first rainy days; it was so huge, I should have noticed the pull of its gravity.

I was amazing again when we loaded onto the plane that would carry us to Vietnam that it was a commercial airliner: Flying Tiger Airlines. I had never heard of the company and decided that it might be "commercial" but likely not entirely "private sector" as it may have done business exclusively for the Army. Nonetheless, it was refreshing to have stewardesses who spoke to us as if we were customers and to sit in padded seats just like regular passengers even if we were all dressed in jungle fatigues.

My seat was too far from the window to see any more than an abstract white and blue brightness. I wished I could have seen Rainier from above, but I expected to see other world-class wonders in the next year. As we settled into level flight over the Pacific Ocean, which even then I had not yet glimpsed, I sat up and looked behind me at the uniformed young men neatly arrayed in rows nine across reaching so far back, I could not see the faces of those in the rear. Based on their appearance, they were a happy lot. I felt, like them I supposed, relief at getting the trip underway. I settled down into my seat and reached for the conventional flight magazine in the seat pocket, just as in a normal flight. But I was not a normal passenger; none of us were. The Hollywood gossip and business news and shopping ideas meant nothing to any of us. It was just coming to me that we were off to adventure. That is why we felt so up, young men about to prove themselves. All that we had known in our lives was on the other side of the shore we had crossed just after take-off.

Our flight was interrupted by a stop in Alaska to refuel. As far as I could tell, none of us expected to be here and most of us found it amusing to go to equatorial Vietnam via the arctic. I understood immediately that it must have been close to a great circle route for the flight but my store of background knowledge did not make me feel superior, only the more stupid for failing to anticipate our route when I had all the facts necessary to figure it out. From the airport, I sent a postcard home and hoped my parents saved it so I could have the postmark. I never expected to be in Alaska and thought I may never get back there unless I stopped again on the way back after my year in Asia. I was seeing the world. I always knew I would one day. It was dark in Alaska when we arrived and I found a window to look through in one of the lounges. I saw nothing but the usual airport parking lots.

After a further fourteen hours in the air, we landed in Vietnam at a base whose name I did not recognize. We were marched into a formation while our duffels were piled on the tarmac. Then we collected our gear and fell back into formation. We sat on our packs in the sun for about two hours. Some of us slept. We took turns going into the small building near us to drink water or urinate. The toilet was the only place that seemed alien. There were cleaning women inside the men's room. It was an unbelievably terrible job, I imagined. The thought crossed my mind that I would rather be a soldier than have their job but I knew I was lying to myself. I waited until the attendant was on the other side of the room before I unzipped myself toward the urinal.

Eventually we loaded into buses that took us away from the urban port to a processing camp in the interior, but there was no announcement of our destination. The name would not have mattered but it would have been nice to know if we would be on the bus for an hour or a day. The buses were in the familiar Army style of OD color and out-of-date styling. I pushed to the front of the line as well as I could to get myself a window seat. I had been napping uncomfortably for the past twenty-four hours and now I wanted to see this famous place. The seats were like the ones I rode in buses to my elementary school, metal boxes thinly padded with a worn cushion. A buck sergeant[11] responsible for getting us aboard made sure there were two GIs in every seat. The last few rows of seats had been removed and we tossed our gear back there.

We soon moved into the scenery I expected, rice paddies and small villages. The villages were especially interesting. The unintelligible writing on storefronts, the populous dressed in loose monochrome clothing and the pervasive and obvious poverty made it clear we had arrived. It did not feel real, more like a newsreel or a cheap travel film, with no plot, no point, and less beauty than I had hoped to find in the Asian countryside.

About an hour into the bus trip, and not far from its start since we travelled slowly and made frequent stops for traffic, I noticed a line of Vietnamese irregular soldiers dressed in black walking beside the road. The two in the

---

[11] The lowest rank of sergeant.

middle of the line carried a pole between them and on the pole hung a man. I realized I had been impatient, looking at the countryside on my first day, to see something memorable and here it was. I elbowed the guy in the seat next to me and silently tilted my head to point out the scene. More than me, he abandoned his façade of casual disregard for the world around us and gaped at the sight. It was reassuring to me that he saw it too. He muttered his favorite obscenity quietly to himself and then sat back with no more than a glance at me. I thought the man swaying by his wrists and ankles must be a prisoner because it would be too uncomfortable to carry an injured man that way although he seemed to be dressed the same as the ones carrying him. It was months later when I remembered this sight and realized it was not a man on the pole, but a corpse; not the same thing.

XVII: Starting the New Life

We awoke to the sound of reveille. I performed the conditioned responses of a grunt. I did not think of jet lag when I heard the noise. I did not think at all. I sat up in my first conscious moment. In basic, we had been told the sergeant would not dump you on the floor if you had both feet there already so I had learned to make that first movement automatically. It was not clear that all sergeants had the same rule but I had never been dumped although many of my peers had.

Something was starting. It was not the glorious promise of college, but I was immensely curious to see what was coming next. A sergeant guided us, almost courteously, to breakfast. We newbies talked among ourselves without saying anything. None of us knew what was coming; none of us had been here before. None of us would reveal any worry. We had all become used to waiting whatever fate the Army would hand us. We ate our familiar fare at long familiar tables. The Army had fed us well since the day I arrived, rumors of saltpeter additives (to lower sex drive) notwithstanding.

After chow, we drifted back to the huge tents where we had spent the night. The sides were rolled up now so they were just canopies, shade from the tropical sun. We had been told to await orders. No one knew anyone and we all sat quietly on our bunks. No one slept despite our jet lag. I was as antsy as anyone and walked a slow, tight circle around the tent where I had been assigned. I could not go far off because I had to keep an eye on my stuff, worthless though it all was. We had no idea what was coming next to us and did not expect to know much. When the Green Machine was ready to use us, we would hear about it. I went around the tent twice and figured that was enough. I wished I had brought a book to read but was also glad I did not have much personal gear to carry and guard. I thought I might watch a card game but there was none in progress. I had not played cards since leaving school. I was not sure if that was because the Army games involved serious money or if I felt cards had played a significant role in wasting my year at school. ...Either way, I had no urge to play.

I sat on my bunk and contemplated writing a letter. The only people I would write would be my parents. I had never written a letter to my siblings and could not see why I would. My mother, of course, would love to hear from me. I could tell her a little about the place, keeping it all upbeat. But that was not the letter I felt like writing. I was not feeling at all upbeat and did not think it was necessary to pretend otherwise. I would have liked to write to my girlfriend, to say how I missed her and that I was not in any danger here except from boredom. I would say I had not given a thought to any other girl since leaving home, since leaving her. I would not expect to even speak to a girl over the next year. I had never seen one in the Army and was not planning to get hospitalized where I might meet a nurse. I would be loyal for lack of opportunity but loyal for certain. ...If I had a girlfriend to write.

I thought of writing to my fraternity pals and would have written them if I had lasted long enough to get into a fraternity. The card players I had known at school were scattered to their various futures and I knew none of their full names and none of them was giving me a thought anymore. The wrestlers were not a letter-reading type. We got along well but did not see each other off the mat. High school friends? I had dropped them when I went to college; that part of my life was gone and held no interest since the day I got my acceptance to my first choice university.

I did not feel especially sorry for my having no one to write and no one outside my family who knew or cared that I was in the Vietnam War. It is just how things were. People liked me on the whole and I was smart and healthy on the whole. I would have a good life when this was over. I would take it all up again a year from now and all *these* guys would be dropped, forgotten, and this part of my life would be gone and no one from it would hold any interest for me.

Oh, there was no denying it. I was in it. I had failed! I was in the wrong place. Those underachieving grades were not good enough. It was my fate to fail for making so little effort, for coasting through life! At least I knew Vietnam would not break me. I was broken before I arrived.

It would be hard for Vietnam to meet the terrible expectations my peers and media and literature had built into me for the experience. Against all odds, as I had assessed them, I had managed to get myself into the place on earth I least wanted to experience. I now anticipated danger and discomfort (which I would not mind much), petty orders (chickenshit), atrocities (I worried more about the ones that might implicate me as perpetrator rather than as victim), possible capture (more dramatic than injury, even than permanent disability), and a certain lengthy delay to getting life back on track (which I would do because I had seen the folly of my ways). In my first days, it all seemed possible.

The tropical weather was just as it ought to be, like Florida in summer. The guys in my tent were a silent bunch at this point, generally similar to myself despite the tawny color of their skin, their Southern or Hispanic accents and their rough humor. I fit in. Those people who said I needed to work more in high school had been wrong. This is just who I was! My destiny had arrived. I had become a part of history, more as data than an individual actor, as my mother had characterized it, as "cannon fodder."

XVIII: I Start to Earn My Pay

My first real duty came on the third day in Jungle School. My squad went out on a patrol. We knew it was not a serious patrol, just one to show us how it is done. We had practiced it before, over and over back in Stateside exercises. There was not much to it, just walking along without tripping over anything and being ready for Charlie.[12] Still, this was Vietnam.

The sergeant who was taking us out was only an E-5, a buck sergeant. That proved further, in my mind, that this was not serious. Later I learned it was common in the most dangerous areas to send out a team under a buck sergeant. They were as expendable as my father had said second lieutenants were in his war. Maybe the difference was not which war I was in. My father had been a second lieutenant.

Our buck sergeant commanded our fullest attention; this may have been a repetition of what I had done in basic training and in advanced infantry training, but it was a full measure more significant and this guy was our guide. He told us the hills we would traverse that day were part of the war. Charlie could be anywhere. We were always being told this but we believed him more than most since we were in the Nam now. He was taking whatever risks there were along with us.

---

[12] GI argot for Vietnamese fighting against the U.S. Army.

He claimed Charlie had been seen on these training patrols. He pointed out that we were already trained, that this only partly a refresher and partly real protection for the camp.

We went through a trace in the coils of barbed wire. He moved a few wooden frames that allowed the wire to be easily parted. He did not explain how this simple system was enough to protect the camp but I guessed that the guards in this part of the perimeter knew where the opening was and would keep a special eye on it. Probably it was mined so they could blow anyone using our easy path.

It was a warm morning, dry and bright. Steep hills with dusky green bushes kept us from seeing far from the camp. We headed up a narrow valley between two of the hills. There was a well-worn path, just the sort of route we had been told to avoid. But when we reached the far end of the notch, the sergeant had us spread out in the conventional manner and we headed across unmarked ground. He appointed a point and told him where to go. I was an out-runner on that first stretch. He identified our first objective, a knoll, not a mountain top, just a few hundred meters on. The squad worked its way up the slope. I watched for trip wires and other signs of booby traps. In our area of operations, nearly all casualties were from booby traps. I walked in a manner opposite to the way of the Indian as described by James Fennimore Cooper. I was quiet, as they were quiet, but I went always to the fresh ground, never on a game trail or any other easy way.

At the knoll, we did not congregate. We stayed spread out so one explosion could not take out too many of us. The sergeant took a new bearing and we passed on to the next objective. I looked back to the camp, part of which was visible from this higher elevation. I thought how easy it would be for Charlie to set up a mortar here. He did not need to have sharpshooters.

We wandered over the hills for an hour and then took a rest, still spread out, and still keeping somebody on guard. We saw nothing and I came back unconvinced that Charlie ever roamed those particular hills, but when we got back to camp, inside the wire, I explained to the stranger nearest me in formation before we were released that it was the most useful training exercise I had in the Army, that I had paid attention as never before in Army or civilian training and he answered slowly with a profound stream of agreeable expletives.

In my second week, I was deemed ready for guard duty. During training in the States, guard duty meant preparing for inspection. The best dressed guard would be excused from duty. The contest was usually won on the strength of someone's brilliantly shined boots. I never got the knack of the spit shine despite Franklin's efforts to train me, not to the degree needed to get out of guard duty, and always served my turn. In the Cha Rang Valley Camp, we had an inspection of the guard, but it was minor, not chickenshit, and no one escaped from duty. It made sense that shiny shoes would not be an asset in Vietnam.

The duty consisted of standing for an hour at a time atop a wooden tower, then taking off for two hours, using one of the two cots in the room under the tower. Then doing it again and again until twenty-four hours had passed. The towers were connected by field telephones so any problems could be communicated to the Sergeant of the Guard.

On my first shift, just at dusk, I looked out on the hillsides I had traversed on my training patrols. From the patrol, I had looked at the camp as a target, as it might appear to a sharpshooter. From the tower, I not only had a different perspective, I was involved in a different game. The tower guards were not looking for anyone in the hills, we were looking for sappers in the wires. Our class on guard duty had claimed the VC sent sappers to crawl on their bellies slowly through the wire, carrying heavy explosives on their backs. They would, we were told, bury themselves in the daylight hours and then inch forward at night. Once inside the perimeter, they would set up booby traps.

I never knew how much to believe of what our instructors told us. I believed they usually had relevant personal experience, but their actual instruction was rote as it had been back in the world, every word orchestrated for them. I did not trust those anonymous authoritarian authors. Besides, every training session on a topic was identical even though the nature of the war differed from place to place. Or so it seemed likely to me. Therefore, I tried to think for myself, in contradiction of all instruction. There being little to do but think while standing in the guard tower, I went back to the logic of the unstructured cops-and-robbers games I had played with water pistols. What was my opponent thinking? What was Charlie seeing? Where would I be if I were him? I slouched against one of the supports that held up the roof of my tower; I was too easy as a target and not much I could do about that. Was it possible to dig into the ground under the wires and hide out all day? I did not question Charlie's commitment. If I had the American Green Machine arrayed against me, I would be desperate and if I had lasted over these years, with a war raging my entire lifetime, I would be dedicated to my craft.

At night it was soon too dark to see the hills, except when a flare went up or when a "mad minute" was declared. Since it was understood we could not see the sappers, we had mad minutes from time to time, and everyone fired into the wire, tracers lighting up the ground in a red glow. We loved the noise and it gave us all a reminder of what our rifles could do.

It would have been a more efficient operation if we had the night scopes we heard about in training. We were proud of our clever economy that could invent a way to see at night and to install it in a telescope. It was a beautiful example of technology developed for the military that also had application for civilians. We were not issued such scopes for guard duty. In fact I never saw one, even during training, but I did learn and remember that it was our responsibility to destroy the scope if we had one and we were about to be killed or captured. Destroying it meant leaving no piece larger than a quarter.

A training post seemed as good a target as any if their goal was to make the war painful for us, rather than to take territory or supplies. Of course the training area might have been sited to be relatively safe but we were always being told no place in Vietnam was safe; Charlie was everywhere. It might be the safest place in the AO[13] and still a good target.

An hour in the dark is a long time. It is hard to stay awake in the small hours, even if a flare goes up from time to time and there are a couple mad minutes over the course of the night. One is nearly forced to think about the

---

[13] Area of operations

situation in front of the guard. It is the best topic for thought as it keeps focus on the matter at hand.

I thought it was my moral duty as an American citizen to contemplate the plight of the Vietnamese and the long, late, cold hours before the dawn were my time for this practice. I wondered which side I would take if I were Vietnamese. No matter how I spun the scenario, I always came up on the side of the Viet Cong. I took refuge in my small knowledge of the situation; accepting that as an excuse for being on the side I was on. Every citizen should not be expected to know as much as our elected leadership and their professional staff. This was the same mental refuge I employed to allow myself to accept the Army draft; not my stupidity or immorality, but the acceptable and understandable limitations of my knowledge. This theme played often through my brain during those hours because it was so unconvincing to me. It was the sort of excuse I had used for underachieving all my young life. It was not a good sort of excuse, and had never mattered much to anyone but myself. Poor information was a less acceptable excuse than usual when the result was to go around killing people. I had enough religion in me to see that.

In addition to worries about my eternal soul, I worried whether the other guards were maintaining a serious vigil. No one ever spoke about the possible immorality of killing our fellow man, but there was a widespread view that the whole war was a waste. This might have contributed to a relaxed pursuit of the war except that the pursuit was already pretty relaxed due to the passive incompetence of most of my colleagues. I trusted them less than I trusted Charlie and yet I had to act as if I trusted them. I looked to the towers on either side of me to see if I could discern any movement, proving someone was awake over there. If I looked long enough, there always was some movement. Someone was always awake.

It was my third night of guard duty, which I understood was probably my last turn at Cha Rang Valley before I went to my permanent unit, when I saw something in the wires. We had a quarter moon that night and no clouds at all, just enough light to believe we could see. It was not a movement; it was a face that I thought I saw when someone fired up a flare. I always looked hard when a flare went up and always saw suspicious shapes. The flares were attached to small parachutes and drifted while they were alight so the sharp shadows they cast were constantly moving. Faces were easy to imagine. Our brains interpret anything close to a face as a face. But this one made me shiver when I saw it. It was small, just the right size for the distance, and it was incomplete, covered on top with something, but it was so distinct I could not deny it. When the flare died down, I was left blinded for a minute so I kept my attention on the spot where the face had been, planning to look again when my eyes re-adjusted to the dark.

We had taken a class in night vision. Pilots, we were told, were especially rigorous about protecting their vision and avoided white light for thirty minutes before flying. The lights in the cockpit were red because there was something about the eye that red light did not harm night vision much. And, of course, I knew that staring at a point of light at night, say, a star, temporarily burned out something in the eye and the point became invisible.

The flares that fired over our barbed wire blinded us completely for a moment and then weakened our vision for many minutes thereafter unless we shaded our eyes, which we never did. A sapper would be wise to make his move right after a flare fell to the ground and fizzled along our barren perimeter as if trying to set the dirt afire. We had also been told in our class that we could see movement better than specific images at night, so as my vision recovered from the flare, I did not stare at any spot but kept my attention generally where I saw the face and I watched for movement. It might have taken me five minutes or it might have been less though it felt like more before I gave up, deciding I had seen nothing.

I gave up but I had nothing else to do and I returned my attention to the spot over and over until I saw him raise his head and show his face again. I saw the movement first. Under these circumstances, we saw lots of things that were not there so I was not convinced. And then he lowered his head and I could not see his face but I could see the small mound of his body. I did not stare, but I was sure the shape I saw could not be construed as a face. He must have moved. For the first time in my Army career, I called the Sergeant of the Guard. It was Simpson, a staff sergeant I knew fairly well, and liked. We called him "Simpo" which did not mean anything and he did not mind. He came running.

He clambered up the wooden ladder on the side of my tower. I showed him what I saw. He could not see it, of course. Neither the face nor the movement was there any more and he had no memory of what it had looked like before Charlie put his head down. But he took me very seriously. Perhaps he noticed that I was rational, well-spoken for a grunt, aware of the problems of night duty. He asked if I could shoot it. I doubted it. Maybe on a good day, but not at night. Firing at him might alert him and he

could escape. We could not direct others to shoot at him.
No one but me knew where I thought he was. I did not
want to shoot up another flare. I asked if I could crawl into
the wire to get closer. "Gung-ho mother fucker!" was his
answer, meaning that it was a great idea.

Simpo went to the other towers to alert them not to
shoot me. I sent one of the off duty guys up the tower but
the second one went up too, just to see what might happen.
I did not want to make a spectacle of myself. I preferred it
to be a matter between me and the sapper. That is how I
had always played it in my imagination: a contest between
myself and the enemy, to win, to avoid losing, not for the
glory of victory.

I began my crawl behind the tower. He would not
see me do this from any excess of impatience on my part.
When I reached the edge of the tower, I realized I could not
see the suspect spot at all from ground level. I backed up,
stood up, and went around the tower to look it over again. I
saw my angle. I looked for a place in the wire I could reach
and that would give me a view of the sapper. Then I went
around the tower and restarted my low crawl.

We had practiced low crawl in basic and in AIT,
always with emphasis on keeping low and being fast. This
night, however, the emphasis was on silence and this made
me slow as well, but not as slow as the sapper was reputed to
go. It required patience and I had more patience because I
was aware it was critical.

The technique we learned had us fold our arms in
front so we could cradle our M-16[14] out of the dirt or mud
and use our elbows to pull us forward. I slid along,

---

[14] The rifle used by U.S. troops.

repositioned one leg into a bent position and slid forward again. It was not silent but it was quiet, and probably would be hard for a sapper to locate.

I could not estimate the time it took me to reach the wire. I tried not to think of the other guards and Simpo watching me. I was not sure I had reached the place I intended but I thought I had kept on track. In fact, I had not gone very far. It was about twenty-five yards to the wire and I added another ten yards of lateral movement. My original plan was to work my way through the wire to get closer, but in the dark I was too unsure of my position and of the sapper's position to risk further movement. I looked along the surface for something recognizable. I was almost sure a certain tangle of wire was the one I had expected to find from the ground. I adjusted my attention on the assumption that the tangle was the right one. Every unevenness in the earth before me could have been a sapper.

I called my opponent a "sapper" rather than the more generic "Charlie" out of respect for his accomplishment in getting so close. I never called anyone "gook." Even my superficial comprehension of the civil rights movement in America was enough to know that was wrong. Neither the white nor the black soldiers in my unit had ever shown such consciousness which I attributed to their not having gone to college.

I shivered from the stress of my situation. I tried to believe it was due to cold from the ground and the hour and the inactivity of lying quietly. With enough concentration, I could stop the shivering, but it was not worth it. No one was near enough to notice it. And when I saw him lift his head and turn his face in a slow arc, my shivering went beyond my control. His head went down again but I could see the lump that represented his body and the one that was his head. Damn, he was as real as my own breath and he was much closer than I expected. He must have moved while I was coming in. But he had not looked at me with any particular emphasis. He might have heard me but not known what the sound meant. His deliberate movements made me believe he was entirely unaware of me.

I slowly, very slowly, moved my rifle into position and moved the safety into the off position, using the constant pressure we had been taught to keep it from clicking. I did not use the sight since I would develop a blind spot in my night vision if I focused on a point for long. And I heard him scraping forward, his forward, not mine. I was almost proud that he sounded just as I did and he was a professional sapper! That thought somehow humanized him for me. He was not really a professional. We had been told sappers trained long for their role, but I doubted he was anything very special at it. More likely, he preferred to be a farmer or a city boy rather than a sapper.

The sound of his movement was clear. He was making very small movements, creating a constant, faint throb. I imagined it was my pulse. I tried to count how many times I shook in my shivering between beats. My shivers were too fast to count. His shape moved closer. I could not miss him at this range, even in the dark. My M-16 was set on automatic. I would squeeze off three rounds, aim again, and squeeze off three more. I did not fear him at all. I doubted he had a rifle or pistol. His only weapon would be a bomb, one that he could not deploy at me. Maybe he had a knife too. I hoped the guards would not respond to the sound of my shots by strafing the wires in panic. Since I had been in Vietnam, none of us had seen a VC[15]. All the guards were new to the country, like me, and they were not likely to be well disciplined. Worry about the other GIs was not a factor though in what came next.

It was disgusting to imagine shooting that human being crawling through our concertina[16]. He must had had a miserable life so far and had poor prospects for improvement, but here he was risking his life, practically throwing it away, to make some small strike against the invaders.

No one could see us. The other guards had no night vision goggles. I controlled the moment. I decided to catch his attention and to signal him to leave. His mission was destined for failure anyway. He could just turn around. There was enough time before dawn to get away. I would hold my rifle on him in case he rose up to attack me or if he decided to proceed with his bomb. Only he and I would know what happened. I was willing to go back to Simpo and say I could not find him in the dark. Maybe in the morning we could find his tracks and everyone would see how close we had been. I could be a hero to both sides. Maybe the VC would have a new attitude about the invaders and see us as more human.

He shuffled closer, and I could see him moving slowly. He was not headed directly for me, but was at an angle that would pass ten yards away. If I were to get his attention, I would have to make a sound. It was probably safe. He probably had no gun. I doubted he had a grenade. There was no reason to equip a sapper with such valuable

---

15 Viet Cong.
16 The coils of razor wire used to protect the camp perimeter.

equipment. I thought of what sign to make. I could wave him toward the way he had come. Would he understand? Not a chance, I knew, not in the dark. I could let him go into camp or I could shoot. Or I could be gung ho and capture him in hand-to-hand combat. He was moving away from me when I fired. Three loud rounds. Then three more. I listened. The silence was thick. No one in the towers shot me. I was not sure I could see him, which bumps in the earth might be him. I saw no movement.

"Give me some light, Simpo!" I shouted. A flare went up a short second later. I saw my VC fifteen yards away, motionless. He was dressed in the flimsy black fabric we called pajamas. It must have been uncomfortable attire for crossing the dangerous and ultimately deadly filth of our stony moat.

"Any more of 'em, Simpo?" I shouted.

A squad with large flashlights came out. Simpo had gotten them ready. My excursion had been monitored as much as possible in the dark. I would have a bronze star for this night. I had won a terrible game and there was no joy in it. I would not volunteer again. The lesson of my father had been relearned.

In my first two weeks, I had accomplished what my father might have wished for my whole tour. I had not gone there to impress him, but it was a nice thing to notice at that moment. I was trying to see something nice in the affair. The songs I admired, the poets of my generation, the culture to which I aspired now placed me with the damned. I did not believe in hell but I knew I was going there and deservedly so. And it would begin with my assignment to the field next week, and the year I was to be in Vietnam would be an eternity if karma had anything to do with it.

XIX: Deployment

I rode along with a dozen other newbies in the back of a deuce and a half[17] to LZ English[18] outside Bong Son, an hour from Cha Rang Valley. There was no canvas cover on the truck so we had a good view of our AO on the trip. We passed rice fields, "paddies" people usually called them but they were dry at this season and just looked like grain fields to me. And we passed through small towns, with garish, hand-painted signs on blocky, concrete shops with tin roofs and garage door openings. The guys said they smelled like nuoc mam[19] but all I smelled was diesel exhaust from our truck. Whenever we stopped, a crowd of children ran out to the truck and shouted "took, took." I thought at first they were begging for candy but it was cigarettes they craved. And yet the two fingers they all held up to us were not a sign of smoking; the palm was turned toward us in a peace sign.

Whenever we crossed a bridge, and it was guarded by Americans, we waved peace signs at the guards who were probably sitting on their helmets and flack jackets. When we crossed a bridge guarded by Koreans, they would be wearing all their issue and give us a firm salute. "Strike" we called them, those ROKs.[20] When we crossed a bridge guarded by ARVNs,[21] we would have to look underneath to find them lounging in the shade.

---

[17] Two and a half ton truck, the Army's usual troop carrier and general workhorse vehicle.

[18] "LZ" stands for "landing zone."

[19] Fish sauce.

[20] Stands for Republic of Korea.

[21] Stands for Army of the Republic of Vietnam.

XX: Overseas Home

LZ English was a broad bowl of a camp, larger than Cha Rang Valley, but with the same sort of perimeter of concertina and guard towers. The only green inside the perimeter was tents, sand bags, or GIs. The rest was hard red dirt. It was a long way from the mountains, probably five clicks[22], but the mountains were clearly visible and gave an orientation to the place. The helicopter landing area was on the side nearest the mountains. It was the most conspicuously busy place. The hospital was on the opposite side, near the wire cages for prisoners. At the bottom of the bowl was the PX[23], the most substantial construction, as if it were the center of the town. Most of the other space was occupied by "bunkers" consisting of large tents with sandbag

---

walls. I was assigned to a squad-sized bunker.[24] We had a wooden door on our bunker, making it feel relatively permanent.

XXI: Isaac

One other newbie had arrived with me. No one else from the squad was around. The other guy was a short, chubby fellow from New York City. He introduced himself as Isaac and as a Jew. I say "chubby." He was too small to be called "fat." Hardly anyone was fat in those days, not compared with now, and fewer still were fat among soldiers.

But Isaac was soft, pudgy; not a good physicality in his present situation. Nonetheless, he seemed smart and self-confident. His urban background seemed to give him some

---

[24] A U.S. infantry platoon usually consists of three nine-man rifle squads and one nine-man weapons squad. Three or four platoons, each led by a Second Lieutenant, make up a company commanded by a Captain.

advantage in social interaction but his ethnicity placed him out of the mainstream. I liked him for his confidence and the ease with which I could understand him, compared with most of the guys I had met who were from class backgrounds and ethnicities even less familiar to me.

We were surprised to find ourselves alone, not tasked to some maintenance or training project. There were three empty bunks. I dumped my duffel on one and asked Isaac if he had any preference. He gave me a long answer that meant he did not. I wondered if he always spoke so much or if it was a symptom of stress. We unpacked our bags into the empty lockers beside our bunks and he chattered on, mostly about where he had his infantry training; mostly complaining about the Army. When my bag was empty, I flopped down on his bunk and asked him why the hell he was there; how had he screwed up so badly as to be where we were. His patter did not miss a beat as he launched into that part of his life story.

He had been a poor student, not as smart as his parents wanted him to be and the frustration of being unable to do very well led him to try less. Yet he had done well enough to get accepted into a third-tier college on Long Island. He was not looking forward to more school, but he was not looking forward to anything else either. And then he found a girl who would have him. They knew each other from school but had never actually spoken to each other. Neither one of them was any prize in the high school lottery and they were both vaguely hoping to meet someone better someday. And then they found themselves in the parking lot outside a school dance where neither had a good time. He had not noticed her at the dance; had spent the time leaning against the wall with like-minded male friends, muttering about the girls they would have liked to know. He felt utterly trite, a paradigm of failed adolescence. So he walked away from his buddies, who were good enough friends in most circumstances but only added to his depression by being as inept as himself with girls, and said something directly to Margarete. It was not anything clever, just something casual, like "cutting out early too?" as if they both had something they needed to do that evening. She had said something he did not understand and walked up close to him, staring into his face in the dim light of the parking lot.

Isaac had been feeling disgusted with himself, with his inability to interact with a girl at the dance and it was, he explained to me, to prove his mettle to himself that he leaned forward and kissed her. The touch of her lips was softer than he expected and much more pleasurable. In an instant, Margarete was a woman to him, not the socially inept and physically ambiguous classmate who had confronted him. They escaped their usual fate to the shadows beside the auditorium wall and to some mutual exploration of young bodies through the synthetic fabrics of the day. They did not speak, not really, not in sentences, although they both uttered sounds that they interpreted as communication. Throughout it all, Isaac claimed, he was conscious of how such encounters were portrayed in movies and fiction and avoided playing like a fictional character. Rather, he tried to be genuine, to do what he had dreamed of doing someday, to the extent his nerve would let him proceed. And when he had exhausted the possibilities of the venue, he took charge again and stepped back to catch his breath and straighten his clothes.

It was necessary to say something kind to Margarete. He was grateful to her and had greatly enjoyed her; he was even hoping one of his friends might spot him standing now in the light talking to a girl in the shadows, even if he knew it was Margarete. Yet he could not sincerely say he would like to repeat the experience with her. Through her, he had learned something; not that a girl could be exciting, of that he never had any doubt. He had learned even a girl he did not like could be exciting. More than this, he had learned he could experience a girl. It was more than enough for one night. He just needed something to say to wrap it up graciously. She spoke while he hesitated. She asked him what he wanted. He said he would have to give that some thought. His answer was not much but at the moment it was good enough for him. Aware that he had not expressed his appreciation, he turned to leave. It seemed cruel, like a Hollywood cad, and he liked that, liked to be the one turning away.

She did not call after him that night, but she passed a note to him in school on Monday. He was embarrassed to read it; it was so juvenile. It reminded him, as if he needed reminding, how immature he was in his sexual relations. He resolved not to give in to the opportunity for a girlfriend he had not sought and did not want. She was not the one he wanted to learn with. He ignored her note.

She knew their social circle well enough to see she was the best he could do and she reminded him of this in her next note, obviously already acknowledging he did not want her. She told people they were a couple. Word reached his friends. It was good to his pride to deny their five minutes of coupling was as important to him as it was to her. That is what he told his friends. He did not quite believe his own story. It had been important to him too, just not the start of a long period of intimacy with her. It had been enough to prove there would be more excitement someday, more than Margarete could supply.

Her notes and the rumors that reached Isaac or that he imagined were circulating about him were very distracting. His senior year did not fulfill the potential he had seen in it when he started high school. He did not suddenly become academically engaged, and he did not discover a talent for something that would earn him money before or after college. He did not manage to find a willing partner better than Margarete and she reminded him of this whenever she could though he needed no reminding to be aware of it. His mother found a date for him to the senior prom, which made him furious, but he went anyway and hated himself for going. He let a few weeks pass after graduation before he enlisted in the Army. He had hardly given a thought to what he might have liked about the Army. He had done it just to get away from Margarete and his mother and the certain drudgery of four years at college.

And how had it turned out for him, I asked with a gesture to the camp around us.

He replied that it had worked just fine. He had felt like a fool when he was being sworn in, and had proceeded because he deserved to be a fool, one among twenty disoriented young men without a self-conscious purpose in any of them. It had been easy, if not exactly pleasant, from there. He was told what to do or was required to do nothing. For the next couple days he thought he was dead already, just waiting for the formalities to end. He had signed the papers.

And then came a moment he had not foreseen, a moment that changed it all for him. The day began in the fashion of the new ordinary in basic training, rising to a racket in the barracks from a drill sergeant in crisp OD long before the sun showed any glimmer in the east. He had struggled as was now usual to get himself dressed exactly right, and to make his bunk to the tight standard everyone else could achieve. No one had spoken to him for two days except for the orders and insults of the sergeant. He was surrounded by recruits but none was quite as alienated as himself. He had no ambition to fit in with the coarse young men in various hues of skin, and unfamiliar and improper versions of English. His ambition extended no further than to get to the end of the morning run, dragging not too far behind everyone else with a minimum of pain in his legs and lungs and on to the next stage of the torture.

He stood in the loose formation after the run, half listening to the ranting of the sergeant about how they were all utterly worthless human beings when the sergeant decided to address him directly. Isaac was not wearing his "blouse," the OD shirt with his name sewn above the pocket, because they had run in t-shirts, yet the sergeant knew his name. He did not know everyone's name but he knew Isaac because he had pestered Isaac so many times for failing to keep up with the others. So Isaac was forced to give his full attention to the humiliation. The sergeant went through a long list of names, a list well honed by generations of military training and modified regularly to keep up with the times. As he ranted on, shouting in Isaac's face so closely his spittle accumulated on Isaac's face and sprayed into his eyes. When Isaac blinked it away, the Sergeant claimed Isaac was beginning to cry and used that to extend his list of insults. Isaac was not crying, felt no urge to cry, but he visualized the figures around him believing the assertion, reducing him even further in their silent opinions. It was not fair. This was not one of his failings. His emotions shifted to a more personal form of wrath; on top of all he deserved, was even more offense.

And then the Sergeant stepped back, proud of his work and addressed the whole company. "Did you see," he asked them all rhetorically, "that I can call Izzie here almost any disgusting thing he has ever thought in his short, puny life and he accepts it? He knows it is all true because the U.S. Army told it to him. But did you see there is one thing I did not call him? There is one thing I will never call this recruit and I will never call any of you. And if anyone ever does call Izzie this thing, or any of the rest of you filth, you will all stand together and resist; you will resist to the max and you will back up Izzie like he was yourself. You are in the U.S. Army in a time of war and don't nobody, nobody, ever call any of you 'boy'." Without a moment of hesitation, he then marched them off to breakfast.

Isaac sat on his bunk without looking at me. He had told his story for the first time. Combat is famous for bringing intimacy to comrades in arms but sitting in a quiet bunker is no combat experience. Isaac had not spoken at length to anyone since he got out of high school and began his steady descent to Vietnam. Once he got started, it poured out of him. I had nodded sagely as he explained it all to me but had not said anything. Telling it made it all clearer to Isaac; it made sense to him for the first time. He was not proud of this life of his, but it was not as absurd as he thought it would be if it were described aloud. And his audience, me, did not laugh. Isaac was prepared to regard me as his friend. "Right on," I told him. It was a popular phrase in those days, a phrase whose meaning depended more on the style in which it was uttered than on any content in the words. My languid tone was intended to show agreement with his conclusions and sympathy for his situation. In truth, I thought he was terribly weak to allow his life to be so thoroughly derailed by two women who should not have had such negative influence at his age. However, I was also well aware that I had no better excuse for getting to this quiet bunker so my empathy for him was genuine.

XXII: Rosco

A few nights later I was wakened by quiet laughter a couple bunks away, where a candle burned to create a dim space in just the opposite way of normal privacy; it allowed the people using the light to be seen by those not of the party, but the intention of privacy was clear and the light was effective in providing it just as surely as if there had been walls around them; thin walls that let sound through, not words with their meaning, just the sound of them and the sound was of relaxed, late-night happiness. "Drunk," I thought. It was not a criticism. They were keeping to themselves.

One voice was louder than the others, louder in the way of a naturally loud voice, not an inconsiderate one. And that voice nearly always derived a laugh from the others. I was simply curious, not irritated by their mutterings. I did not recognize the sound of him, yet another person had joined us and the group's intimacy and the late hour suggested he belonged in the squad. I leaned up on one elbow to see who it was, to see who had come in. He saw my movement and called out to me in a stage whisper. "Newbie, newbie," was all he said.

I answered "Follow me." That is the slogan of the infantry. It was a good joke to pretend it had any meaning. He answered "Rosco." It was a kindness on his part to recognize me like this, me being a newbie. They liked to pretend that being new mattered. It actually only mattered for a few days but was recognized for longer. They took the privilege of being more veteran far less seriously than fraternity brothers or officers did. Rosco, I already knew, was popular although he had a little rank. He was the buck sergeant in our squad, not enough rank to alienate him from us.

I did not seek out Rosco in the next days; I did not seek out anyone; but Rosco was hard to ignore. He was big, noisy, clumsy and endearing. He always had a smile on his broad face, not self-conscious about being a black man at a time when that was cause for showing pride. His friends, or maybe it was just the soul brothers in the squad, kept trying to tell me about him, as if he were a prize they had won. I was excessively aware he outranked me and I did not wish to appear to be cozying up to him. Nonetheless, his story slowly came through; that he had been away because he was getting married; that he was marrying one of the stewardesses he met on the flight to Vietnam from his R&R[25]; that he was already married to a woman in Ft. Bragg.

---

[25] Rest and relaxation. Within each one-year tour of duty, U.S. soldiers were given two weeks at an R&R post, such as Bangkok, Singapore, Hong Kong, or Sydney.

One had to be impressed by that story although it was never told or embellished by Rosco himself. The usual pattern was for one of the brothers to throw his arm around Rosco's shoulders and start the story as if I had not heard any of it before. As one of the two newbies, it was not unreasonable to assume I would be uninformed. They did all enjoy the story so. And Rosco ate up the attention like a Broadway actor except that he had no lines.

The longest things he said were "right on" or "there it is," both affirming phrases without actual content. I might have heard him once say "all the way," which is the slogan of the airborne. Although he was an E-5, I did not hear him say "follow me." I do not mean that I never heard anything else from him when his story was being told for him; I mean that I never heard him say anything else ever in the nine months I knew him before he rotated back to the States.

Of course, with so little detail coming from him, his story was very thin and I never believed it. The Army knew if you had a wife, I reasoned, since they sent her a check every month. And he would have to let the Army know if he were getting married in Saigon. I doubted it was even possible to get married while in Vietnam, but there was doubt in my mind, only in mine. The Army surprised me over and over so I dared not be certain about anything.

Rosco was such a nice guy, I did not want to question his story, not even when I was alone with Isaac. I thought the story might have been like a magician's patter: no one really believed it, but it kept everyone's attention when he was around and we never noticed he was incapable of articulating a sentence or even an original or major phrase.

XXIII: Settling In

By the end of that first week at English, I had learned what a refuge the bunker, the hooch, would be. No officers bunked with us. We smoked cigarettes all the time; drank beer whenever we wanted. Money was meaningless. We had enough for anything we could do here and did not save for tomorrow. Some hooches smoked weed. You knew which ones they were since the sweet smell of marijuana is hard to hide. I understood you should not go into one of them except by invitation. I wondered what the guys who were assigned to one of those did if they were not into weed. There were not very many head hooches, as far as I could tell, not like the reputation of GIs in this war. Sometimes the 'Ps[26] would break up the head bunkers. I was never into that scene and did not know what punishment came with a raid. I heard there were some guys who smoked heroin because it did not have an odor so you would never be caught. Besides, heroin was cheaper.

XXIV: Dump Guard

Our first formations showed me things were going to be more relaxed than in my various training camps. No one inspected our uniforms. Everyone wore his uniform, but I had the feeling that was because they had no other clothes rather than anyone requiring it. They were wearing various military caps, unpolished boots, wrinkled clothes that might not have even been especially clean. It was like Peter Pan in Neverland with no petty rules on personal

---

[26] Short for MPs – military police.

hygiene, as if all that training and humiliation were for some other assignment, some other place.

At an early one of these formations I was assigned to a garbage run. It sounded like bad duty to me but everyone assured me it was good, better than anything on the base but shit-burning detail. That sounded implausible. KP[27] would have been the worst assignment apart from going to the field. Alternative duties might have included guarding the armory, the Brigade headquarters or the Company quarters, fire watch at night, or any number of special assignments within the base camp. Guarding the camp perimeter, as I had done on my big night at Cha Rang valley, would have been an assignment for the whole company when its turn rotated around.

Shit-burning detail was, surprisingly, exactly what it says. We had two places for our bodily refuge and were constantly being warned to use them for health reasons. One was piss pipes, exactly what their name says. I wondered if the pipes sticking up from the ground

---

[27] Kitchen police, i.e., working for the day in the kitchen.

at an angle were meant as a game to attract us to their use, just to limit the number of places for urination. The outhouses were for defecation. There was no pit beneath them, just a bucket. And every day someone had to burn it. This required collecting all the buckets assigned to the shit-burning detail (the name of this task was never shortened, such as to "S-B" detail), pouring kerosene into the buckets, lighting them afire, and stirring the mess so it burned thoroughly. How is this not a terrible assignment? It was always done by papasan, never by GIs. The GIs assigned to the duty paid one of the older Vietnamese men waiting around for any kind of work. The going rate was a quarter. The GI was expected to monitor the task to be sure it was completed well. It seemed terribly inappropriate to pay a Vietnamese to do one's assignment, even if it were not a disgusting one. Whatever ethical issues arose in this arrangement had been worked out well before I arrived.

My garbage detail was loose-marched to draw weapons. I presumed these were needed for personal protection since we would be going off the base. Our deuce-and-a-half was already loaded by the time we reached it. It was not in bins or bags, just every kind of refuse piled together. To me, it felt like a joke to ride shotgun on a dump truck although I saw there was some slightly higher status for the armed guards relative to the detail that had to load it. I had no idea then how close my role would be to that of a stagecoach guard. Maybe if I had thought about the life or living standards of rural Vietnamese I might have anticipated the forces at play on a trip to the dump. My training had not prepared me for what I saw.

I rode on the back with two other privates, but I was the only newbie. We climbed on top of the load, and each spread out a flattened cardboard box to sit over a dry patch, weighting it down so nothing would blow off the truck. It was fun to ride up high with the breeze of the truck's movement. The casualness of my colleagues reassured me that the road was safe although the scenery was quintessentially Vietnamese and therefore looked threatening since I knew such scenes only from the news media. We passed flooded rice paddies with women in flat, conical straw hats bent over in the water, replanting rows of light green seedlings. The far sides of the paddies were bordered by bamboo windbreaks and the profile of steep mountains lay behind that. I had seen something like this and even some villages on the bus trip to Cha Rang and the trip to LZ English, but the view from the bus was not nearly as sweeping and completely lacked the sounds and odors of our ride atop the truck's load. I did not notice the garbage odor much. I did notice the diesel exhaust from our truck the most, and in the years since then, the smell of diesel takes me back to transportation in Vietnam. But I also noticed the unfamiliar smell of charcoal from the households with a cooking fire and, sometimes, the reek of nouc mam, the ubiquitous, odoriferous fish sauce which, I was told, was being aged in the small sacks hanging beside the road. Whenever we passed children, and we passed many of them, they waved two-fingered peace signs at us and screamed out "took! took!"

As we approached the dump, the other two "guards" stood up on their cardboard platforms and warned me to be ready. As usual with newbies, I knew nothing and was not told anything about what was coming. I did not even know we were approaching the dump. As the truck slowed to round a curve, Vietnamese boys emerged from the bushes and ran alongside us, trying to clamber aboard. My colleagues shoved them off. Now they explained: the boys were not allowed on until we entered the dump because they would throw things off the truck to their partners and it would make a mess. We passed through an unguarded barbed wire gate and stopped. Suddenly we were overrun with boys. The other guards let them on so I backed off. They started sorting through the garbage, collecting selected items in piles.

We drove on another hundred yards to the edge of the largest mountain of garbage I had never seen. It was an unreal, cartoonish surprise that spoke of excessive productivity and/or underutilization. A lingering look revealed it was roughly sorted although there were no workers visible. Old tires were piled in one place, broken boards another, small appliances formed a small industry of their own. Everywhere there was torn paper and nondescript vegetable matter. The odor was disgusting but not overwhelming. It was something to be avoided, tolerable for the duration of our stay. The rest of it was a wonder, a surprise for my trip to a war-torn country that the most unusual thing I see is the utterly pacific trash pile, run by imps in tatters, ever covered in sores and filth, unlikely to mature even to my tender age at the brink of adulthood. I was the privileged race here. No way to feel sorry for my lot as a near draftee.

The three of us clambered down and waited for the boys to clear out the truck. They shouted to each other, arguing over the spoils. A small army of girls surrounded the operation, sometimes collecting things from a boy, sometimes offering to sell us a Coke. One of the guards asked me if I wanted to screw one of the Coke girls. They looked like they were ten or twelve years old, but he said any of them was available. They would ask for five dollars but could be had for less. You could bargain for what services they would do. I was disgusted by his suggestion and by the leer on his face but even more by imagining the existence that would motivate these girls to this level. I looked out into the rubble. It was a village. Right amid the trash were caves and huts, some occupied by children apparently cooking something. No one at the dump was much into his or her teen years, like another bizarre Never-Never Land. For the first time I had a sense of how the Viet Cong could recruit their young guerrillas to fight with their minimal weaponry, sparse clothing, and inadequate diet against us with our modern military might.

XXV: Donevan

The E-6 from the next bunker spent a lot of time in our quarters. He came in with Rosco, both of them loud and friendly. We did not mind him; he was probably just what the Army needs in an NCO.[28] Donevan knew the manual but before you knew that, you knew he was sharp from the way he wore his uniform: well pressed when on the LZ with his cap folded and creased into a signature shape. He had that urban cool some black men wore in those days.

One of those first nights it was time for chow but there was no formation; no one to tell us to eat. Isaac and I started talking in low tones about what the schedule might be. We watched the others to see if they were collecting somewhere, expecting a formation. And then Donevan

---

[28] Non-commissioned officer, i.e., a sergeant.

came by to say he was going to dinner at the club and asked if we wanted to go with him. We had not even spoken with him directly before and did not think he especially wanted to hang out with us. And two of his buddies from another unit were standing at the door waiting for him. He was simply a good guy who was aware that we were disoriented. Or maybe he had been assigned to orient us, but I preferred to think it was the former.

We followed behind Donevan and his buddies, who were chatting actively among themselves, past the mess hall to the NCO Club. During training, I had never gone to the NCO club and had assumed it was for NCOs. In Vietnam, at least, the NCO club was for all enlisted personnel; not for officers, of course. We stepped into a large, dark room with tables scattered about without any pattern of arrangement. Chairs were also scattered around, not necessarily near any table. There was a curtained stage on one end and a long bar across the opposite side.

Donevan sat at the bar in one of the three remaining stools, but he turned to Isaac and me to see what we were doing. We stood to the side hesitatingly and Donevan got up and pulled a couple tables together and then he called to one of the beautiful Vietnamese waitresses, although no one but me ever called them that, never called them "waitresses." They were usually just called "girls," which they were not if we were not "boys." We sat at the table and the waitress came up to us and asked what we wanted. Up close, she was even more beautiful in an exotic way, extremely slim, graceful, nicely made up and confident. I did not want any alcohol; I wanted dinner, so I just turned to Isaac to let him answer first. He was at a loss too and said he did not want to drink. Donevan did not appear to be listening, but he heard Isaac and spun around on his stool. "They've got food and shit." He pointed to a hand-lettered sign above the bar listing three kinds of steaks and a choice of beans or fries for sides. I had a ribeye done rare with fries and a Coke, one very fine dinner.

Donevan only had beer, as far as I saw that evening. He did not drink heavily. He leaned on the bar while the smoke from his cigarette curled around his head and he ignored the talk from the two sergeants who had come in with him. He just seemed to be listening to the music. It was country and western. I knew very little of the genre. I turned it off whenever I could. It was not bad, just not something I would call my own. I had liked a few country ballads when I was too young to know any better. And I enjoyed listening to "Patches" and "Calahatchi Bridge" that I heard on the radio while I peeled potatoes on a hot day back at Ft. Polk, Louisiana. I would not have admitted I had enjoyed them if I saw any of my friends from home.

XXVI: Dan-Boy

"This here's Dan-Boy."   I was asleep when I first heard his name.   Swanny was introducing me to him anyway. He repeated the introduction whatever number of times was required to get me to comprehend his purpose. When I finally responded rationally, Swanny said I was to take care of him and then he left the hooch. Swanny put us together as if we belonged together. Maybe it was because we were both white, the only white ones in the platoon other than Isaac and Swanny. And Swanny did not expect me or anyone else would go around with Isaac because he was Jewish.   I doubt he even considered the possibility that another Jew would turn up. Swanny was sure he did not think any less of Isaac for his being Jewish but Isaac's background was not forgotten for a moment. Swanny was not that way with everyone; he just was not familiar with Jews. If there were any in the town where he had lived his whole life, he had not heard of them.

I had been on LZ English just three days when Dan-Boy showed up and already I was being asked to be the guide.   I liked being a newbie with an excuse for not knowing how to act. Someone told me it applied for three months.   They pretended the title of "newbie" was derogatory but no one really believed that. Everyone had been new sometime. Being a newbie just meant you had a longer time to go before rotating back to the States. Only the truly mean-spirited ridiculed the naiveté of a newbie. That newbie would be a colleague in arms soon enough and those were ever respected.

Dan-Boy turned out to be the guy I would most remember from my military years. He projected health with a straight posture and a firm handshake. He was not overly tall, but was barrel-chested and lantern-jawed. At our first meeting, he was quiet, but friendly. I pointed out the unclaimed bunk for him and sat on the bunk next to him while he unpacked. I explained how relaxed discipline was among the grunts, except, I assumed, when actually engaged in the business that had brought us to this place. I did not talk long; there would be time to absorb it all. More than that, I did not know very much more than he did and I did not want to pretend otherwise.

After my little commentary on what it was like, as far as I knew, and a little on the other guys in the hooch, none of whom were in at that early hour of the day, probably all at breakfast, I suggested we go to chow. He sat on his bunk, apparently wanting to soak it in a little before doing anything. His sour look was comforting to me. I was willing to admit this was a terrible place to be and provided my own sour look to comfort him.

I asked where he got the name, "Dan-Boy." It was surely not given by his mother at birth, not formally anyway. I thought people ought to be given nicknames, distinctive ones anyway, rather than announce them to a new community as he was doing. I could have hung onto my "Skinny-Quick" moniker and would have liked to have a nickname, but I had left it in the past, awaiting a replacement that would have meaning in my new surroundings. "Dan-Boy" seemed pretentious or infantile-- I could not tell exactly. I was learning in the Army that there were many more cultures in America than I had met before.

Dan-Boy was from Georgia, a place where it was more common to have a double name from an early age. The practice felt to me like a cliché from an earlier era although it was hard to see any harm in it. He had graduated from college, from the University of Georgia. It was, to my mind, a lesser school than the one I had left, although all I knew of it was that it was in the South. Yet it was obviously more prestigious to have graduated from a southern university than to have been expelled from a northern one. I would have to regard him as the most educated person in our platoon. I was getting used to being more educated than the people around me, reassured that my college career was in remission and inevitably would resume triumphantly, and it hurt to be beaten by a Southerner. But I saw it was not Dan-Boy's fault. He did not show any particular pride in his degree.

He did have pride in his body. Since he was obviously very fit, I asked him what sport he played. I hoped he would return the favor and ask me what I played and I would modestly let out that I had played a lot of sports and been a highly successful wrestler. It would surprise him because I looked gawky when I was, in fact, "wiry" or "rangy." I expected he had played football and had used up his sport with nothing to show for it but his thick neck. He surprised me with his answer. He was a body builder. I knew nothing of the sport but regarded it as disreputable, dominated by drugs and vanity. A body should be the result of its functions rather than built for looks. I glossed over the memories of trying for brief periods to build my body into something better looking. I was not sure if it was rude to ask if he had competed in body building. He might have only meant he was a weight lifter and used a term I associated with a pseudo-sport. I was pleased that he took no offense at my question even though he was not a competitor. He said his goal had been to get a 20-inch difference between his chest and waist. He claimed that was some kind of very high standard. At his best, he did not quite make the 20-inch mark. I had been thinking of him as thick and only when he made this comment did I see he had a narrow waist. There was a rumor among boys, young men, that body builders were not as strong as they looked, and that they were not flexible enough to be good at sports, but I never believed that. He had wonderful muscles and they must have been useful. He posed briefly in profile, not in a boasting way, but just to show me his project. And then he surprised me even more by saying he wished he had not looked so unusual.

He told of a day in his last year of college when he went to a dance at school and a group of drunken guys started to mock him. Their words made no sense; they said he looked powerful, as if that were a problem. Drunks often make no sense. They were jealous although Dan-Boy had not claimed he was anything more than them. Maybe he was standing too proudly. He did not take them seriously until they met him in the parking lot. They beat him until he was unconscious. After that he got a gun and carried it at night.

XXVII: First Patrol

I had been in-country for just over a month when my first real assignment came along. I was starting to wonder at the inefficiency of it all, that I had trained for so long, been equipped and transported and processed, and did nothing to further the war effort other than a bizarre event in Cha Rang when I was supposed to be just acclimating to the place. I was not terribly interested in contributing to the war effort since I was not clear on what we were trying to accomplish, but I did object, as a citizen who would someday pay taxes, to the expenditure in me and in my peers without more of an effort at a return.

Against all expectations, Vietnam was becoming a bore. LZ English was not big enough. I felt confined because I was confined. A few guys (utter fools to risk everything on empty sex) did slip through the wires to go into the vil to find a woman but most of us, like myself, had just the one circular dirt road we could traverse in ten minutes at a brisk pace. In the middle of the circle, in a deep dip that should have filled in like a lake but never did, were the NCO Club and the PX. Outside the ring road were the places where I had no business: the hospital, POW pen, motor pool, airport, the last really a heliport. I had no occasion to meet anyone outside my

company so all those tents and supply buildings along the road were meaningless to me.

I overheard conversations by troops from other units with rumors of adventure as in the movies: encounters with the NVA[29], napalm called in, a collection of ears secreted from the officers, prisoner capture, gruesome injuries given and received, abuse of lithe young women who spoke no English, kills made and kills falsely recorded. I did not believe all of what I overheard or all of what was repeated back in my unit, and not a word of it was attractive in any way and yet I was ready to get into the field. I had already relaxed any objections I had to the war so much as to be where I was; I had given up my right to make decisions to my officers; my soul was as bloody as their deeds. This was not to say I had no self-respect. No one but me would ever both know and remember how honorably or not I spent my time here, except those who had stood beside me, complicit in whatever I would accomplish in the many remaining months in this place.

Where had I been? Dix first, then down south, and then to the far coast of America and past Alaska, I had arrived in a hot, wet, rugged, insect-ridden country whose only inhabitants I met were sassy waitresses in the NCO Club, minor players in the biggest event in my nation's experience during my biggest experience of life so far. I was in a place too strange to dream, where family and seasons and love and art and education did not exist. I was both more free than I had ever wished to be and more tightly bound than I could endure. I could drink and swear and use drugs and stay up all night and have crazy sex with

---

[29] North Vietnamese Army

prostitutes without consequence. And very possibly and very soon, I could kill someone and be congratulated for it. That day was due and it arrived in my fifth week.

My first trip outside the wire in a real combat zone was a Thursday. It was not a simplified version for training purposes, since there were only four newbies among us: Isaac, Dan-Boy, me, and Lieutenant Romero, together constituting more than half the white men in our unit. The latter was a second lieutenant[30], the rank my father had said was the lowest in the Army. It was a joke he liked to tell on himself. What I heard in my war was that the grunts would not respect a second lieutenant because they had no power. Second lieutenants could not complain up the line that they have been disrespected because they are supposed to command respect. And they do not have enough experience to command. And they have officer's privileges so the grunts with field experience enjoy disrespecting them. That was what I heard but it is not what I saw.

Romero was pretty good and we all could see it. He was not petty, not chickenshit in my father's terminology. He was better educated than any of us and did not do anything stupid. Like all officers, he was apart from us. We did use any nickname nor even call him by his last name when speaking to him directly. For the most part, we did not care about him and he cared about us only to the extent that we did our jobs. Besides, his relationship to us benefitted from the lingering truth in my father's myth. The VC, or whatever enemy we faced in the war of the moment, targeted officers and second lieutenants were closest to the

---

[30] The lowest rank among officers but formally ranking above all sergeants, specialists and privates.

front. In Vietnam, we wore "subdued" insignia, dull colors and metal of rank to make it harder to target the officers and we did not salute them in the field for the same reason. Romero successfully conveyed the sense that he was not telling us what to do so much as communicating what he was required tell us. Responsibility lay somewhere higher up, with someone we had not seen and never would. Unless, ours being a democracy, responsibility truly resided with all of us.

Twenty of us checked in with the guard tower at dawn and followed a guide through the wires. We did a radio check and hiked off toward the line of hills where mortars had fired toward LZ English a few times a day ever since I had arrived. We were to find the route the VC were using to get into the range of our LZ and find where they were taking cover from our retaliatory artillery strikes. It was said that they could afford to send out a team of two to fire a couple of mortars and then lose the two to our retaliation, that the fortune we spent on artillery was worth it toward their goal of breaking America's will, but I did not believe that. I believed what we had been told over and over in training by veterans of this war: that Charlie was good at it. It took us a certain predictable amount of time to locate where he had set up his mortars and just when we could fire back, he was gone. We never found any bodies, nor his lost equipment.

The strategy we faced and the strategy we employed were not matters of gaining ground. Charlie attacked our willingness to fight. He did this by making it expensive for us as much as by harming our soldiers. And he targeted the attitude of our troops, never good. By the time I had arrived, it was depressive. I knew no one so angry as to consider fragging[31] his officers, nor did I know anyone who thought the war was accomplishing anything positive.

There was an attractive element to the way we headed out. Soldiers were not cool at this point of American history and the symbols of the military had been depressingly pressed upon me from the moment I began training: short hair, uniform clothes, rigid formations, obedience, suppressed creativity; none of which was apparent in the mission team. We all wore OD but no two wore it the same way. Some wore standard issue baseball caps with a variety of folds to reshape them. Some wore boonie caps, like fishing hats with a small brim all around but in camouflage fabric and decorated with ammunition stuck in the brim. Someone had an OD handkerchief tucked under his hat so it hung on the back of his neck like a Bedouin. Half of us had some of our shirt buttons open. Donevan was, typically for him, well assembled. His boots were bloused as for a parade. His sleeves were rolled up with mathematical precision. His cap was turned to a jaunty angle. I stole a few looks down the line of troopers; it was just as it ought to be, as it would be someday in the movies. They were hard-core. Not me; I was a newbie and looked it. What is more, I felt it. I had no urge to look hard-core. My uniform was regulation in content and styling. As I had for the prior several months, I had consciously enjoyed making no decisions about my clothes. In this, I did what the Army told me to do and appreciated the simplicity of it. I paid close attention only when putting on my socks and tying my shoes as I did accept the Army's warning about

---

[31] "Frag" refers to a fragmentation grenade, a rumored means of removing particularly obnoxious officers.

taking good care of my feet. I worried a little that no one else was as concerned as me about feet. The Army was right about their importance in our line of work.

The line of troops marching loosely out of the LZ which included me as a member made me feel like a spectator. Isaac and I did not look like the rest of them. Possibly I was preparing to meet a woman who cared how I dressed in the field. I dressed to be myself within the constraints of the wardrobe; nothing too cocky; that would be indefensibly immodest. I had lacked the guts to wear bell bottoms in college yet I imagined every day during college I was dressing as if I were going to meet a new and groovy woman. In Vietnam, the number of men had declined precipitously in recent years however the chance of my meeting a woman to woo on our mission was infinitesimal. I was prepared to fire my M-16 or launch a grenade upon a native of this foreign land if told to do so but I was no brute.

Past the narrow no-man's land surrounding our camp were rice paddies. The crop was being transplanted at this time. I did not understand much of rice production, but it seemed the seeds were originally strewn at a certain density and the seedlings had to be replanted to a lighter density. It required a terrible amount of mindless work, bent over in standing water, i.e., walking with rolled up pants in mud under the tropical sun. Their slim bodies and flat conical hats lent an exotic peacefulness to their appearance. We walked single-file along the dirt banks between fields. The mama-san[32] farmers ignored us as they did the crows, or

---

[32] Term used by GIs for mature women. The suffix "san" is used in Vietnamese to indicate respect. "Papa-san" referred to mature men.

their local avian equivalents.

By the time we were through the paddies, the sun had cleared the bamboo windbreaks and beat upon our backs. The land sloped up to a village. It was the sort of village that had no shops, not even a paved road. There were specialized buildings although I could not tell exactly what uses they had, probably some for grain storage, tools, or firewood. No cars or trucks were visible but a motorbike was parked by a few of the huts. I had only seen young men ride motorbikes when I was on the main roads but no young men showed in this village. Small children with no shoes and, often, no pants, stared at us but no adults acknowledged our presence. I wanted to wave in a friendly way at someone but the kids who watched us did not respond. They had no concept of interacting with us. I almost made the motion of taking a cigarette from my mouth and mime the word "took," but I did not want anyone to think I was really going to give a smoke to them.

Romero told us to stay away from the buildings. This little place was not a target of our mission but it could be harboring VC. I did not know if I believed he was serious. We were right next to the base. Why would anyone take such a risk? But I knew nothing of why these people did anything. I suspected Romero was just trying to scare the new or the gullible ones among us, and amuse the experienced ones. I did not want to be seen as gullible but I did not care much what any of these companions thought of me; my goal was constant, to get home again and every caution worked toward that end in my mind. Curiosity was for another time and place.

Maybe I should have been more of a tourist going through the village because we soon entered a dreary second-growth forest and hiked the next two hours without seeing any variation in the view. It had all been cleared to make charcoal. The brush was too low to give any shade and the sun only got hotter as it got higher. We stayed off the many trails though this heavily used area so the footing required some attention. Furthermore, we were climbing gradually into the hills so it was not an easy walk. Finally we came to a stretch that was actually steep. It was deeply eroded and the loose, gravelly soil gave poor traction for the climb, but it was worth the extra effort to get somewhere.

We stopped on the ridge and looked over our shoulders to see a view back to English. The air was uniformly thick, not a fog rising from the paddies, not a smog from the roadway, but a muggy haze that made the base seem far away. We could not see the farmers toiling in their fields because the bamboo windbreaks hid the low lying area from our view. I had not noticed when we hiked out that the LZ was on a small plateau. English was easy to see although its edges were softened by the humidity and distance. The canvas and tin tops of our bunkers and buildings were out of place in the green landscape. Our guard towers revealed the nature of the base. The barbed wire perimeter was invisible from where we sat. The village we had seen was also invisible.

The lieutenant assembled us to review our mission. We would sweep across the slope looking for signs where a mortar might have been set up or where the mortar team might have hidden. Our first priority, however, was to be alert for signs of booby traps. Charlie would have known we would search this area someday.

"Dan-Boy, don't you think Charlie is way better at hiding his booby traps that we are at spotting them? I mean, I think even I could set one up no one could see."

"So, Skinny, you have to step where he does not think you will step." All right, I had told Dan-Boy what I was called during training.

"That'll be *on* the trail, right? They always tell us to stay off anything that looks like a trail. Charlie knows we're told that, right?"

We sat on the rocky outcrops as long as we could without Romero getting too worked up. It was not as comfortable to rest as we pretended. We were young and fit and not tired. The sun was not as hot as it would be later and the lather on the back of our necks turned to a clamminess we had not noticed when we were active. When the mosquitoes found us, despite our sitting in the sun, we were more than willing to go forward with the mission.

Dan-Boy had found a bamboo pole somewhere along the hike here and was using it to test the ground in front of himself. He did not check all the ground, we were not mine sweepers, just the places he was about to put his foot. It was a good idea and I wondered that the Green Machine had not institutionalized the strategy. I also worried that there was a reason for not adopting it and I did not get myself a stick. I did not trust the Army exactly. It was inept in a thousand ways, but it was marvelously experienced in making war and the method for sweeping a hillside was part of that.

We spread out along a line Romero drew in the air. Actually, he sliced a vertical plane with his open hand. For some reason never explained to me, not when I was paying attention anyway, the military did not point with a finger, it sliced a plane that intersected the land to indicate a direction.

Our recon this day was very much like "police call," which was the act we repeated after every extended break during training-- lining up and walking over the area where we had taken our break to pick up any trash anyone had dropped. Cigarettes were "field stripped," scattering the tobacco to the winds and rolling the paper between our fingers into an insignificant ball. Mostly we smoked the cigarettes the Army issued us in our C rations, without filters, but if you found a filter, you put it in your pocket until you came to a trash can. If you found a live round, a bullet, you immediately turned it in to the sergeant in charge. There was a time during AIT when someone in another unit found a round and fired it, apparently for the fun of it, and shot someone down the line. Having gone through Army training, it is not as hard for me to imagine someone as stupid as this. Shooting that damn rifle is just too much fun for some trainees.

"Meathead!" Dan-Boy called to me. It was not my usual nickname but we had an understanding that any rude name he might utter would refer to me, so I grunted an acknowledgement. "Numbnuts," he continued. "Think they have any rattlers in this here country?"

"I don't think so, Dan-Boy," I answered. I always answered his rhetorical questions. We both knew there were no rattlers in Vietnam. We had all paid attention when the subject of poisonous snakes was taught. There were some bad ones, they claimed. I had not really learned how to recognize them; it did not matter as we avoided all snakes. There was something known as a "two-step" because you would get no farther than two steps if it bit you. Because I loved nature, I paid more attention than most during this class and remembered it was known more formally as a "krait." Knowing this word made me seem to be an expert whenever the subject of snakes came up. The two steps sounded like a myth, but I did not have any way or desire to test it.

"Skinny, I don't see you," Donovan whined like a drill sergeant. What he meant was that he was the next person in the line to me and that I should be close enough to him at all times to see him so we would know the ground between us was being inspected.

"With all due respect, Sergeant," I called back to him, "I'm not all that good looking that you need to see me all the time."

"I don't need no newbie stepping on something and getting hurt so much we got to carry you out of here."

It was not a logical argument exactly. Seeing me would not prevent me from stepping on a mine, but I got the idea behind it. More than ensuring the mission was done well, he was watching out for my safety. I was not sure why he would make me his project, but I did appreciate it. There were dangers out here I did not comprehend. He saw Isaac, Dan-Boy and me as the new guys, the ones who might need to be guided, and I could not say he was wrong although I had liked to think I was carrying my weight. I adjusted my steps in his direction until I saw him. He was looking toward me and I waved to him.

"Don't stare at me, Skinny. Look where you thump those big flat feet."

I did look where I put my feet. I was more afraid of stepping on a booby trap than I was of being seen by Charlie in ambush. I had heard plenty of rumors from the field and knew booby traps were our main threat. I did not expect to find one in this area near the base camp which had been trampled many times before on missions just like my own.

Dan-Boy came up with an old rusty affair that was likely an old booby trap. He called Donevan over to look at it before he touched it. Donevan saw right away that it was old and maybe broken during construction. He said it was designed to drive a bamboo splinter into an American but it was not operational. It was not hidden effectively and not even designed with any explosive material, just a tin can, a spring and some wire in addition to the bamboo dart. Dan-Boy asked if there was any danger in taking it home. He was more interested than me in having a souvenir of what he had faced in our quiet form of combat. Donevan was oddly adamant about destroying it in place. "Don't leave anything for Charlie to reuse," he emphasized although that was not an answer to why Dan-Boy should not take it away as a souvenir. It could not be construed as an atrocity like collecting ears or a danger like a live round. Donovan was typically serious in adding that he had seen one like this before and it was no toy.

The day took on a pattern of short periods, exactly fifty minutes each, like classes in high school, meted out by Romero between ten-minute breaks. Each fifty minute period, like classes in high school, was more tedious than the one before and they stretched on interminably even though the end was measurably in sight all along. Unlike school, each period was sweatier and filthier than the one before and the tiredness was physical as well as mental, and the mental was mainly stress. This was not a task where boredom was acceptable though it crept in with the invariant terrain and scrubby vegetation of the long hillside.

Eight hours into the mission someone found something. A call came from a sharp-eyed buck sergeant I did not know, although I had heard he was on his second tour which implied he asked to be here. That rumor was enough information to assure me I did not want to know him better. His call at the moment was apparently a happy one. He was too far off for me to understand what particular profanities he was yelling but I got the idea that he had found *it*. I further understood that he was to be regarded as heroic for finding *it*. When I finally heard what he had found, I had to admit he had accomplished something. Was it just luck or was he actually better at our task than the rest of us? Most people said his surviving into a second tour was evidence of his luck. Soldiers are as superstitious as baseball players but I saw only cold odds aided by preparation and equipment. Somebody was bound to survive untouched and it just happened to be Sgt. Gung-ho. His being the one to find the compressed earth where a mortar plate might have been fired... that was his talent, maybe his experience at work too. It worried me when I thought of how this job we had probably did require skill and that enjoying the work, like enjoying wrestling, made one better at it. It worried me because I hated being here. Not the mild discomforts of life in the Army in a tropical clime, I hated myself for being here; for failing to earn a place in mainstream America; for bearing a huge blotch on my cool, on the wrong side, the short-haired side, of youth culture and; more and more, for trying to be the instrument of death to Charlie who would never have cared to do anything to me or anyone I knew if I had stayed on my own side of the Pacific Ocean.

We were ordered to stand our ground while the Lieutenant observed the compressed earth. Fortunately, I was near the thing and managed to drift over to get a look. Romero probably had no opinions of whether the patch was really an artifact of our enemy or just a place where a charcoal maker ate his lunch. He had more training than I did, certainly, but he was almost as green as me and certainly more ignorant of such field marks than most of the grunts on our expedition. He did not show any ego and asked Sgt. Gung-ho to explain what he had found and what it implied. The idea was that this was a remnant of an attack on our LZ and that Charlie probably had a hiding place very near to prepare for the barrage of artillery we would send in response to firing his mortar. They usually had only one mortar set up and fired off three or four rounds, knowing we could not respond fast enough to stop them, but we would get something back at them soon thereafter. Their lair needed to be within a minute or so of the compression mark. That included the delay caused by carrying the mortar away.

Romero called in our location, set up a perimeter and told the rest of us to systematically go over every square foot within 300 yards. Wouldn't you know Sgt. Gung-ho would be the one to locate the tunnel? Having found the compression area, surely we were going to find the tunnel, but it was still eerie that he made the discovery.

I did not get to see the tunnel entrance. I heard it was not easy to spot. It was somewhere higher up on the hill and behind me. I got word to wait for orders and then, sooner than I expected, I was assigned to a place on the new perimeter Romero was setting up. Someone, maybe a few someones, was going in the tunnel. He would blast it with a concussion grenade first. In the confines of a tunnel complex, that would likely kill or incapacitate any VC there. Then that someone, a slim someone, would go inside. My mind was with the tunnel rat rather than my guard duty, especially when the call came down to us: "Fire in the hole!" followed by the wump of a grenade I felt through my legs. I was alert for small arms fire or some other response from the tunnel but there was only silence. No further calls, no cheers of discovery, no sobs of despair, no counterattack from below; not even the call of a magpie or whatever corvid fills that niche in Southeast Asia.

After fifteen minutes of anticlimax, I settled in on a flat rock alongside a wide area of barren, stony ground. It was not high enough to make a proper seat, one that would take the weight off my legs, but it was as good as I could ask to find in the field. The rock was warm, yet not as hot as it would have been when the sun was highest. I propped my back against my pack. I could not move to a better support and still see my field of fire, the zone I was guarding. It would not have mattered as we did not expect any threat to come along. I was really just waiting for the tunnel to be cleared.

"Nice moon," I said to Isaac who was close enough to hear me with a speaking voice. The moon had just risen and showed clearly as the sun was falling low on the opposite horizon.

"The moon doesn't do much for me." Isaac answered after a delay. "It is too close; too easy; too easy to understand. The stars are another matter entirely."

"I don't see any stars," Donevan noted. It placed him in the conversation. I could not see him but could tell about where he was. From my perspective, his voice came through some bushes. Maybe if he moved, I could see where he was exactly.

Isaac continued, "The light from the stars takes years and years, more than our lifetimes, more than the lifetime of our species, to get to us. So what we see is more than ancient. Who knows which ones have died out already?"

"Trite, Isaac." I answered. "That's what twelve-year old boys talk about on their first camping trip, before they are old enough to talk about girls."

"Well, I'm amazed at them anyway. Stars, I mean. Girls too, I guess. They're different kinds of amazing."

"Goddam. Don't make me listen to this!" moaned Donevan. "Seeing that moon is OK but the rest of it! Issac, grow yourself a pair!"

Isaac was undeterred. That is how he was when he had something in his head. He did not care if the guys around him thought he was square. He was content to be square.

"No man, I did not get to the point yet. I mean, of course we all know the light from stars is old, and we can imagine things are different out there than it appears to us. But what concerns me, what I think about, is the light from us going out to them. I've got, what, seventy, eighty years on this planet? We're just getting started you know. We have sixty years left to make our mark. Don't you wonder what you will do in that time?"

"Sure," Donevan answered. "I think of all the women I can have in that time."

"But, you see," Isaac would have us take his rap as seriously as he did. "It's not much time to make a mark and then enjoy it. The great people of history, some of them, did not even know they were great. The people who wrote the classics, Shakespeare and people like that, might have thought they were good, but they didn't *know* if their work would last. Napoleon thought he was great but he did not last. The judgment of time only comes after our time."

"Who cares?" I asked, not having warmed to his topic. "If you are just trying to depress us by saying we have no chance of succeeding and knowing we succeeded, you need not have bothered. We are depressed to the max by being here in the now."

"I'm not depressed," Donevan asserted. "I'm serving my country. Nobody's messing with me. It's not raining on me. There ain't no gooks around. I outrank you college boys and I got the biggest dick in the company."

"So I'm thinking my legacy exists in a sphere of time expanding out at the speed of light from here to the end of the universe. And the thickness of that sphere is the time it took to create my legacy. And the importance of my contribution will be the brightness of my sphere."

"I haven't half the good news Donevan has, although I am ahead of him by having this nice warm rock to sit on, so I have a right to be depressed and I don't see how sending out my legacy to the stars makes it any better."

"In your whole life, you won't have a bigger legacy, Mr. Isaac, than this war you're in now," from Donevan.

Isaac answered quickly. "I hope to do something more than this sitting on a scrubby mountain taking orders from the likes of you, looking for Charlie all day and never seeing him except when his mortar pops on my head on my day off."

"What are you going to do then?" Donevan asked. "What'll you send to the stars?"

"I don't know. I'm not going to write a play like Shakespeare. I know that. I can already tell I won't be the one to discover the cure for cancer either. But I will do something. I will matter to someone. Do my job, you know. Get married and have kids. My kids will light my sphere after I'm gone."

"This war won't be *my* legacy, Donny." I was bothered by the idea of owning it. It was an appalling truth. "But, then, I don't care about having a legacy. Once I'm gone, I'm gone."

"You don't have any choice," Donevan reminded me. "You're doing it. What else you gonna do this big?"

"Isaac thinks having kids would be bigger. At least that would be something I did on purpose. Your legacy has to be something you decided to do."

"You don't always have kids on purpose, you know."

"Well, I would. It's not hard to control that," Isaac said matter-of-factly.

"Donny, you think this war is going to make some kind of difference? Something to remember other than soaking my OD blouse with sweat and losing some of my friends to Charlie?" I asked.

"It'll mean a whole lot to Charlie," Isaac inserted immediately. "However it comes out, he's gonna lose a lot more than any of us."

"The gook ain't gonna lose any more than I already lost. Not the ones who survive. My buddy Smitty had my back and then he was blown away and there's nothing I can do about it. I didn't ask him to take it for me. Didn't have to. I'd rather I took it for him. You don't get to choose. Your legacy is what you left behind. You got to go on with whatever comes out."

"But is it going to matter back in the world a hundred years from now? Or fifty years from now when we're still around and some new war is on TV?" Isaac still wanted to know. He cared about his legacy.

"Fifty years away?" I asked. "When our children are grown, their children won't even know where Vietnam is or was. Five years away this war will be old. It will be out of fashion. Songs will just be about teenage sex again. Back in the world, what we're doing today already don't mean shit. There's no camera crew with us and there's nothing for it to see anyway. Just sitting on some rock in the sun watching the moon come up. My draft board's already forgotten about me. How many people back in the world are celebrating Smitty's legacy? He was before my time, Donny. How many people here are still thinking of him other than you?"

Donevan did not answer which meant the answer was "not many." And Isaac did not defend his claim to a legacy of some better ilk.

"Depressed yet, Donny?" I asked and he did not answer that either.

XXVIII: In the Club

A huge red sun rested briefly on the low mountains as the choppers came in to whisk us back to the LZ. I saw two sunsets that day, once while waiting my turn to clamber aboard and again, from a higher viewpoint in the chopper as we were going back.

We debriefed while kneeling on the chopper pad. The debrief ended too late for regular chow, but the Army promises three squares a day and had set aside some kind of fare for us. No one I knew went for it; we were all off to the club for steaks, fries, and beer. There were canned beans in red sauce for anyone who felt the need for a vegetable.

Dan-Boy and I picked up dinner at the window and then sat at the bar to eat. There were tables available but the bar felt right. We did not have anything to say when we sat down, however, it was good to have company. I watched Donevan sitting a few stools away. He was alone and thoroughly enjoying a cigarette, savoring the taste of the smoke and letting it rise slowly from his lips past his face, like a tiny psychedelic show. I wondered if he had taken some drugs before coming in to the bar.

Soon Mai came to us and asked if we would like something to drink. She was really the reason I wanted to sit at the bar, why I always sat at the bar. We ordered a beer each and she was nice enough to stay with us for a little banter beyond ordering the drinks.

"We doing country and western tonight?" I asked her.

"Manager say there many E-6 in here tonight." I knew what she meant. The career soldiers, the enlisted ones who had stayed in long enough to reach the rank of a platoon sergeant, were usually from Southern, rural backgrounds. Dan-Boy was from Georgia and favored country music but he would not speak up for it since it would mean alignment with the lifers.

"Tell him youth came in the door," I suggested.

"OK, I put on some white boy Iron Butterfly," she teased, knowing I did not like that either. From the suburbs of New York, my taste followed the guidance of Cousin Brucie: Beach Boys, Four Seasons, and Motown. Woodstock was about to take place in August, still six months in the future. She turned away to get our beers.

"I never saw her talk to anyone before," said Dan-Boy with admiration for my familiarity with her. "That one is always minimalist. She's so damn beautiful, she'll get more tips than any of them without any personal contact. Never saw her have any conversation. How did you ever get her to like you so much?"

"I wish. But I do talk to her."

"So why does she talk to you? We all try to get her to linger," and he drawled out that word, "but I never saw her give in."

"If you want to know how to reach the most beautiful girl in the room," I leaned back on my stool and paused for dramatic effect, "don't ask me for advice. What do I know? I never had a girlfriend. I had a few dates, but I don't know how to show interest. I have interest; plenty of it, but it just seems too stupid to say anything about it."

"And yet Sally has talked with you and was comfortable doing it."

"Nice, isn't it? But her name isn't Sally; it's Mai. Vo Thi Tuyet Mai. Same as the First Lady of Vietnam."

"I never had a real girl either, you know. ...There was Sandy." Dan-Boy stopped there.

"Yeah, Sandy. What about her?"

"People thought she was my girlfriend. Maybe she even thought it. Maybe I did. We made out. We went together for two years. Even had sex a few times. It was pretty nice, the sex I mean. But, damn, I didn't love her at all. She wasn't my type."

"You have a type? I used to think I did. I thought I'd like big tits, you know. And kind of a tom-boy style. Nothing like Mai there."

"You didn't know about Mai."

"Guess I learned something there. But I still don't know much about her. I know she won't be coming back to the world with me."

"She could do that. It happens."

"Not with me. I wouldn't do that to her. You know how hard it would be for her back there? Knowing no one, speaking her GI English, and more than that, having no cultural base.”

“There are plenty of Vietnamese in America.”

“I am not prepared to hang out with them. You know, maybe this is why she likes me, to the extent she does. She knows I’m crazy about her but I don’t get to know her, don’t try to advance myself.”

“So she thinks you are a loyal husband to someone back home?”

“No, she knows I’m not married. She knows I don’t even have a girlfriend.”

“How does she know that?”

“She asked.”

“C’mon man, you don’t need to marry her. Just be with her here. You got to know, at least, if she could get into it.”

“I get the theory. I don’t want her that way. I don’t have to marry her, but I can’t just get that close for a couple months at most.”

“It’s a war man! Happens all the time; just doesn’t usually happen with someone as nice as Mai. She’s not a prostitute but she could use some kind company.”

“She ought to have a Vietnamese boyfriend.”

“There may not be so many of those available right now; not the nice stable kind anyway.”

“You think I would be doing her a favor? It is me that could not stand to do it. If I got into her, talked to her one-on-one, touched her, felt her touch me, met her family, how could I leave her?”

“Yeah, I see what you mean.”

"Wouldn't happen anyway. She might like me as the least threatening guy in here or as a ticket out of the war, but I am way too ordinary to be with her."

"Sorry to say it, but I see that point too. Still."

Mai came over to them and took up their empty plates.

"You been away, Churchkey?"

"Not far, Mai."

"I no see you yesterday."

"And I am very sorry about that, Mai. It was like a day without the sun."

"Who's "Churchkey'?" asked Dan-Boy.

"I am. I carved one out of wood and when I gave it to her I told her that name for it. She's always opening beers so she should know the name."

Mai took the carved can opener out of her pocket and put it on the bar in front of Dan-Boy.

"It doesn't even work," she said and pushed it with her finger as if it were a small animal that had just died.

"I beg your pardon, Mai," I offered. "It works on wooden cans."

Mai did not laugh. Dan-Boy was staring at her as if he did not hear anything. She picked up the carving and put it back in her pocket.

"You talk about me? I think I hear my name."

"You heard me dreaming, Mai. Don't take it too seriously."

"It's okay, Churchkey," she answered. "Nobody serious in here."

Donevan called her over and ordered a whisky and Coke. She served him and then moved down to the next customer. Donevan slid his drink along the bar and sat next to me.

"Follow me," he said; the slogan of the infantry.

I nodded in his direction. He leaned on the bar and looked ahead, facing the shelves of hard liquor. No one spoke for a few moments. Ray Charles came on the club stereo. The three of us listened to him sing "Georgia."

"Is he makin' you homesick, Dan-Boy?" I asked.

"I was homesick before I came in here," he answered.

"I've never been to Georgia and he makes me homesick for it."

"Shhh," said Donevan. "Let him finish."

We took his advice and then he asked me, "How do you know Sally so good? Nobody knows her."

"That what Dan-Boy says. Guess she just likes 'em innocent."

"I can get you into her vil. She can't live far off. It can be done."

"Sergeant, you are a man of many talents and we do love you for them. But it would not do me any good to get to her vil. She is already all I can take with this bar between us."

"Time to be a man, Skinny. She's waiting for you. I can see it clear as can be. You can't say no to that!"

"No," I said as distinctly as I could pronounce a single syllable. I slapped him on the back and stood up to leave. "Mai, give me my Sergeant's tab, please." Donevan did not look up from his drink. "Can I put one more on the tab?" I asked him. He nodded "no" and took out another cigarette.

On the way back to the hooch, Dan-Boy said he admired that I was willing to admit I could not handle a sexual relationship at this point. I did not like the way he characterized my position but I did not want to argue about it. He was probably right. What was surprising was that I had been honest enough to give him that impression. I only answered "You gotta be who you are." It was my finest night in Vietnam.

XXIX: Rumors

Rumors were bound to proliferate in late January with Tet approaching. The major North Vietnamese offensive associated with that holiday was a year previous. We had been told back in civilian life that it was the beginning of the end of the war because the offensive had been defeated and the North Vietnamese had expended all reserves toward it. There was no official analysis of it given to us grunts but we did not see it the way it had been portrayed in the news. To us, it demonstrated the North Vietnamese could win a major battle here and there, at least. According to the rumors, the risks guys like us had faced were perceived as small in scale, a booby trap or small ambush. A patrol was not in danger of losing as a whole, just a man or two. It was rolling the dice with the odds in one's favor on any particular roll and slightly against surviving unharmed through an entire tour. But Tet showed a different story, more like the pitched battles of World War II in which the strategy of generals played a role. No amount of caution would be sufficient in such a battle to avoid the traps and no amount of individual luck would be sufficient if your general or colonel or major was having a bad day, for we understood their luck fell on guys like us.

We were told in official briefings that there was a small chance the North Vietnamese would try something again on Tet. Presumably the date was important culturally, perhaps important because of the success their news reports claimed for the previous year's initiative. At my level, Vietnamese culture was a very vague variable.

Thus we were on particular alert that night. Officially, we had been told there was little likelihood of an attack but to keep on our toes anyway. I was in a guard tower looking over a wasteland of coiled razor wire. Just before one AM, a message came through from the Sergeant of the Guard that there was no Tet offensive this year and we would have a mad minute to celebrate. At one o'clock, we started firing tracers into and over the wire.

I was frightened for a few seconds when light came up from over the whole camp. No one should have been firing in that direction. The light came from the flares we used to signal when we were entering the perimeter. We would say on the radio where we were in relation to the camp and then shoot a flare above us. They floated down on a small parachute, providing light for twenty or thirty seconds. Hundreds of them were going up all over. Obviously we did not like to turn in the leftover flares when we came back from the field, as required. We made a good show of our defiance. Reminded me of my bayonet.

XXX: Overnight

By April, going into the field had become routine for me. I cannot say I was jaded, but I was more relaxed than formerly. I was more deliberate in my fears, choosing which ones to obey, based on a stronger sense of which were most relevant. I had seen injuries and been near, not right next to but near, some deaths. I had built up a real but irrational sense of safety rather than a superstitious sense that I was waiting my turn. My comfort was not borne of faith in my expanding expertise, I told myself in playing a game to keep myself alert. I also told myself every mission had been different and every one going forward would be different so I should not rely on my few months of experience to prepare me. And yet there was much the same in my missions: discomfort, danger, drudgery.,, the slow passage of time toward DROS.[33]

It might have been the more boring because I had so little influence over the major decisions. As a grunt, I went where I was told to go and did what I was told to do. They never asked me to do anything I could not or would not do. It was mechanical. It was mechanical for me. Some people did feel stressed. They did not often talk

---

[33]Date of Return from OverSeas

about it although Isaac did. But I could see their relief when we were on the way back to base and see the famous fatalism that guided them through danger, and see their reliance on drugs or alcohol to pass the time until the next mission.

My first trip in April was to last two days. My own fatalism was so advanced that my only active hope for the mission was that we would not have rain during the night. I had less hope of my prayers having an effect on what violence we attracted than on the weather.

In our briefing for the mission, we heard the usual rumors about NVA being in the region. The rumor had not proven true so many times, I wondered that we bothered to shudder in fear any more. The implication was that a relatively large, relatively well equipped unit might be in the area. It was no more frightening to me than facing the nearly invisible VC and their unmanned traps which had inflicted so much upon my unit, my friends and colleagues. We knew about the Tet offensive of '68, that the NVA had proven its strength then, but I did not trust the officers who briefed us; they would lie to us, tell us tales of a bogey man if they thought it would motivate us. For my part, I felt an irony that I needed no further motivation. Their disrespectful lies, their training in leadership, their command voice, their college degrees did not matter-- merely superfluous. I would go where they ordered me to go. I would go if it was VC or NVA or just a hike in the tropical heat. My enthusiasm did not vary with these minor distinctions about who might be trying to kill me.

We packed the night before and underwent inspection. We rose well before dawn and ate a full breakfast, anticipating a couple days of light meals. If you muttered "goin' out this morning" to the KPs serving, they would be generous in their portions. It would have made me sleepy except that I had a second cup of coffee. The activity and excitement of starting out might have been enough to keep me alert anyway. We were loading onto Hueys[34] thirty minutes after chow, quick for the army where waiting was our most common use of time. I supposed it was good that waiting had been a core element of our training.

The sky was gray and the air cooler than some days. We could not see the sun rise by taking off, but the chopper ride always picks up one's spirits. With the doors open, the chopper gives the open view a bird in flight would see. More than a mere bird, we were whisked off to a destination essentially selected by the most important people in the most important country in the world. The effortless power of the machine, the speed we attain, the noise that isolates us from one another, the exotic countryside below, the coming danger...

We landed in a small, sloping LZ after taking a couple turns over the area we would recon. Swanny was our leader and he was on the radio with the chopper pilot during the flight. He knew what we were doing, at least for the first part of it.

A dirt trail ran through the LZ. Where it emerged from the forest was a small shrine on a pole. We marched past it in silence. The path was well worn around the shrine.

We had no friends among the Vietnamese, mostly we thought of them as the enemy. We had been cautioned many times to suspect them all of being VC. The few we

---

[34] A certain helicopter.

knew in some way were outside their culture: girls at the club, the massage parlor, cleaning our boots; and a few old men who did the worst of the work around the barracks. Out here, off the LZ, in the rural area that comprised most of Vietnam, the people were traditional, not weirdly so, commonly so, like my parents who did what they had learned from their parents; who went to church, enjoyed meals with the family, celebrated life's major steps, loved their children, worked hard, and complained about the government just enough to deny responsibility for its actions and inactions.

The shrine was tiny in relation to the war, a talisman of impotent people. I supposed the people were Buddhist. I knew almost nothing of the religion. I knew Buddhist priests had burned themselves in protest of the war or some aspect of the war. I had been in my freshman year of high school and amazed that anyone could be so dedicated to principle. I saw that it was more courageous than going into combat although no one but me seemed very impressed. Of course they might have all been, or some of them, been as impressed as me and merely as silent about it as me. I could not recall anyone in my church with such conviction, not in the most recent thousand years. I was wrong about that. Among the many courageous Christians there was a Quaker who immolated himself on the Pentagon lawn to protest the war. But Quakers were fringe Christians and there was only the one Western immolation against the war. My religion was better known to me as the one that told me I was not, and could not be, a conscientious objector.

By mid-day, the coolness had departed and the pale gray had darkened into an overhead charcoal and lowered into certain rain. The rain held off but we all knew it was coming. We sensed some kind of metaphor relating the threat from god and nature to the threat from our fellow man, but none of us was clever enough to articulate it. Maybe only I felt the metaphor but it was so obvious it had to be present in everyone at some level.

In the early afternoon the wind kicked up swirls of dust that caught me in the eye. From there, it quickly built into a broad, sweeping storm, roiling the clouds so close above us and whipping the thin treetops. We no longer worried about walking quietly, we could not hear our own footsteps in the wind which only made it the more obvious that we could not hear Charlie if he came near. Of course his tactics did not typically have him tramping through the forest looking for us. He might be transporting equipment south through our AO; that was possible. Maybe that was why we were traversing this sector. Our strategy was almost completely unknown to me despite the briefings I had been given. I looked for the parts that were relevant to me and hung on to those, letting the big picture take its own course. They were not trying to convey the big picture to me anyway.

I worked my way close to Swanny and suggested it was not good weather for our mission. I had a few arguments lined up to present to him. He usually listened to me, but this time he broke in quickly and answered that it was great weather for our mission, that Charlie would not be expecting us, that Charlie thought we were soft and likely to jump back onto our choppers when a storm comes in.

Once he had made his decision clear, I could only defer to his rank. I knew well that this was not the place to challenge leadership. Just as I had accepted going into the Army on the basis that those in authority must know more than me, I accepted that Swanny must know more than me. I knew so little.

So we went through the afternoon in a group depression: no close calls, no enemy contact, no natural beauty, no exotic cultural sights, no personal insights, no adventure, no pleasure except the passing of a few more hours toward our separate returns to the world.

We did not bivouac until it was nearly totally dark. We would have no fires and no light so it was best to shorten the time before sleeping. We set out Claymores[35] to protect us in the night and then prepared our dinners. Dinner did not take more than ten minutes to prepare and eat although we tried to drag out the process. We were tired from the long day, but we were young and relatively fit so we would recover quickly.

Swanny put me on the first watch. It felt like a complement to be singled out by him for a position of responsibility although it was odd to feel like that. Everyone would have his turn. Being first on guard is no honor, just a random selection. It made me wonder if I was desperate for approval. Why should I care about the opinion of any of these people? They were not from my segment of society; I would not know them in the future; I was just visiting their segment while recovering from the effects of my rampant immaturity at school.

Only one of us was on watch at a time, which seemed unsafe to me, but not unsafe enough to interest me

---

[35] Claymore antipersonnel mines are small explosives that can be laid out to fire small metal balls in one general direction when fired by a tripwire or a remote trigger.

in lobbying for everyone to get less sleep. With one on duty at a time, we would only lose two hours of trying to sleep.

By the time everyone but me was settled in to some sort of relaxed posture, the wind had slackened enough that I was more aware of the volume of rain rather than its direction. We were not on the cusp of the monsoon (if they had monsoons in Vietnam) or the verge of a typhoon, a fear I now abandoned although I had not been aware it was lurking in my subconscious. It was merely a drenching rain, a discomfort insufficient to make history. The night was warm, not warm enough for complaint, warm enough that I could be wet on my sleeves and cuffs without shivering. I tried to see if my breath showed but it was too dark to tell. I blinked hard to get myself to focus on the task of guarding instead of worrying about my comfort. Without sight, I had to rely on hearing to sense any approach of danger. My hearing found a din of falling water, so steady it was more a background in my brain than the world outside me, so loud I could hear nothing else. I looked for another sense to help me. Smell, maybe. I knew the stink of Vietnamese cigarettes unless those cone-shaped, hand-rolled wads of weeds were better termed "marijuana." They would not smoke when on patrol, no more than we would. The sense of touch would serve me too late to do any good. What was the fifth sense? Taste, my least impaired asset tonight, but entirely useless.

The background hiss made time drag even more slowly, just as darkness did. I had been on guard many times and knew its boredom and the danger of sliding into a stupor waiting for the time to end. Some people claimed that pain helped, like squeezing a nail into the palm of the hand. I suspected it might keep me more alert, but I would not volunteer for pain; my system was more purely mental; choosing one thing to keep me on duty, like peering systematically into each direction of the compass rose, and then trying another thing when that was too boring, like advancing a fixed number of steps in random directions until I worked my way back to my starting point. Coming up with new games to play with myself, games that kept me guarding, was the real game.

My shift on guard finally ended. I woke up Ralph, amazed that he had managed to achieve a deep sleep. He was not angry with me; he accepted his fate was to stand guard now. I waited for him to take a leak and then get into a position on our perimeter, just to be sure he was wide awake. I looked to his posture. He was not leaning on anything too comfortably, however, we had all learned long ago to sleep on our feet.

Then it was my turn to sleep, though I dreaded the challenge. In the dark, I could not tell where the ground might be flatter or softer or drier, but I suspected it was all about the same and none of it any good. My cami-quilt[36] was tucked safely in my pack and I was dedicated to extracting it without getting it wet. For all the luxury its rarity and silky sheen provided, once wet, it was worthless. I made a tent of my poncho with myself as pole and took out the quilt, carefully keeping it bundled up. Then I squatted down inside that tent, shrinking it and collapsing it on me. I drew my knees up to get my legs inside the "tent" and arranged the sides of the poncho to shed water along the seams. I pulled my head inside the poncho and spread the hood over

---

[36] A light quilt with a camouflage pattern often in short supply among troops on the field.

the neck hole. Then I slowly unwrapped the quilt and worked it around me. I could not see anything, but I imagined the pattern on the quilt and took comfort in its artistry. Every other piece of cloth in my kit, from socks to shirt to underwear, was plain OD. It was enough comfort to forgive the rough ground under me. I leaned back on a bush that gently cradled the weight of my torso. I might have smiled at my own talent. As a final gesture of preparation, I cleared my lungs with a languid sigh.

"There goes the neighborhood," said a voice nearer than I expected. It was Dan-Boy who did not sound sleepy. My muscles relaxed, one-by-one. I watched them give way from the tension of the day until I nearly stopped breathing. The first watch was not good on such a night.

"Dan-Boy, how'd you screw up so bad you ended up here? You'd been doing things right, straight and all."

"Just lucky, I guess."

"No really. I've been looking for a chance to ask you. It seems all of us more or less asked to be here."

"You didn't ask to be here. Big deal; you played cards in college. It shouldn't mean you gotta go to Vietnam."

"That's the way it works. But you went to class, studied, did your homework."

"And then I graduated and they snatched me up. That's the way it works sometimes."

"And what are going to do when you get out?"

"First, I'm going to grow my hair out some. Not past my collar. It don't have to be that long in Georgia. I'm going to sell cars. My uncle has a dealership in Toccoa. I worked there during the summer; worked on the cars, but the money's in sales and he gave me tips all the time. He makes six figures. I could be there in a few years."

I whistled, albeit softly, to show my admiration. He had a plan, a realistic one.

"Come a long way from Georgia, Dan-Boy."

"Still a long way back to Georgia, too. I think I can make it."

I did not have anything to add so we went back to trying to get some sleep. The rain came harder and then less hard, proving that time had not ended so morning would come along eventually.

I woke numerous times and adjusted my position but never regained consciousness fully until I could discern some light in the sky and knew it was time to get ready to leave. At that point I was hardly covered by my poncho, having slid four or five feet from my original nest and leaving a trail of slimy OD rubberized canvas and sopping cami-quilt. My pants were soaked through, and my knees were stiff and cold. But my chest was nearly dry since I had managed to keep it covered through the night. I stood up and brushed off, smeared off, some of the mud. I rebuckled my belt, and stretched a little, bending forward to touch my toes, then twisting my trunk and, finally, rotating my head in all directions to work out the kinks in my neck. I was ready for some breakfast and did not feel bad.

Swanny came around and spoke quietly to each of us, getting us going, checking our ammo and the cleanliness of our weapons. He made sure we all ate something. We ate standing. We did not speak to each other much. The noise of the rain made us want to raise our voices to be heard but we did not want to be heard by Charlie. We munched our tasteless, gritty gruel in complete camaraderie and yearned as one to get moving again, loosen our legs and move the day toward its conclusion in a breezy chopper back to base.

Swanny briefed us before we struck out. We were entering a free-fire zone. I did not look at the faces around me but I knew this news had some of them smiling and some more tense. Free fire; shoot anyone you see. I had heard of charcoal cutters being knowingly shot for the fun of it. No one in my squad would do that, I hoped. It was thrilling to some to have this power, these dangerous machines in our arms. For others, the news was simply a further statement of the depths to which our condition had fallen. It was so hazardous ahead, we should consider anyone as our deadly enemy; no civilians, priests, medics, or red cross personnel were in our immediate future. It was Charlie or nobody.

It would have been a comfort to believe I was firmly among those who did not like a free-fire zone. The threat it implied, that we had passed into anarchy, was not what most occupied my thought. I was more troubled by the thought that my unit might kill someone who was not a threat to us. When I realized the source of my concern, I hoped it was a sign that I was becoming more of a pacifist. I had been worried that I was not sufficiently opposed to the war. I wanted to be part of the protest movement when I got back and it would serve me well if I really believed in it. I was pretty sure I was not a true pacifist. There were too many convincing scenarios in which a war might be needed. But I might be able to get behind a protest to this war. I would no longer be confusing my moral position with my fear of being swept up in the draft. But my experience in the war was not giving me much additional information about the war's validity. In fact, I was falling farther behind since I was getting no news beyond what came within my line of sight. Did I have any reason since swearing my oath in Hartford to believe the authorities in my country were any less likely to be serving the public good? Of course I had nothing to add to the thoughts that led to the dead end before I accepted the draft. But I was feeling a little more responsible for the war, for the execution of public policy, more of a citizen. And herein I felt an irony, a moral failure no amount of authority could override. I had been compelled to serve the state's mission, a particularly nasty part of it, but I was not a full citizen. I was an adult, old enough to be told to kill the enemies of my country and to be placed in the line of fire, but not old enough to vote. This was a line I could use to make my case for opposition to the war. It was weak, being less than rigorously moral and being sort of a technicality, but it was irrefutable logic. I stored it in my subconscious to be reworked another day. Maybe there was another unsuspected argument lying out there to help it along.

For the first hours, we maintained the tension. But by our second rest break, the rain was gone and we were steaming ourselves dry in the tropical sun and thereby rejoining humanity. A crust of mud crackled over my pants. Now the driest parts of me had become the wettest; my underwear was damp and rode up where I preferred it were not. I thought back to my training period and admitted it included a good lesson about keeping dry feet (when possible), so I changed into my dry socks and hung the damp ones onto my pack. Since they were OD, they would not make it easier for Charlie to spot me.

We went on, taking our turn on point or on the outside of our small formation. We found no one to shoot, no suspicious trails, no booby traps, no smoke, no human sounds, no distant glints of reflected sunlight, no tracks until...

"Incoming!"

I had heard the "pop, pop" an instant before and hardly believed it was "incoming." Like everyone else, I dropped to the ground although the sound was too small to feel emotionally threatening. We had trained with explosions, never with distant AK[37] fire. Then I remembered an exercise we had done in training in which rifle shots were fired over our heads so we could practice distinguishing the sound of the rifle from the sound of the bullet breaking the sound barrier as it decelerated. Supposedly, it was possible that these sounds would be on opposite sides and make us think we were being attacked in two directions. On the range, I never quite got the difference in sound and out here, all I heard were irregular, unthreatening popping sounds, apparently all from the same general area.

At least their noise was giving me a direction to avoid. All I could see was the tall thin grass around my face. My cheeks felt the dirt and pebbles underneath it. The grass was too sparse to provide any cushion. There was an odor to the soil, a familiar scent, but more intense than I had noticed before; probably because I was breathing dust into my nostrils. While remaining consciously and painfully pressed onto the earth, I rolled my head around one way and another to see if there was any cover nearby, "cover" being defined in terms of the direction of incoming fire. I

---

[37] The principle rifle used by the Communist forces was the AK-47.

thought there was a small depression to my right and I rolled into it. I felt safer for the moment and began to listen to the voices around me. They had been shouting from the first, but I had tuned them out. No one was claiming to be hit. That was good. I kept quiet since I did not know anything. Swanny was asking if anyone could see the shooters. Donevan claimed there were only three or four shooters, but he could not see them either. His guess seemed right, I supposed, for the amount of noise they were making.

This led in my mind to the question of why they would take us on. Were they trying to pin us down until another force could move into position? Maybe there was a mortar unit setting up. Maybe they were moving us into a minefield. Maybe there was an equipment depot being emptied nearby. The only idea that seemed solid to me was that we ought to get the initiative, not be reacting to whatever they were doing.

"There's only four! There's only four!" someone was screaming. "We can take them out. Return fire. Aim good."

That was not the way to think. This was not a medieval siege, sheer numbers were not critical. We were not going to trade casualties until someone ran out of troops, out of cannon fodder. We won our battles with technology. They won theirs with local knowledge, like what terrain surrounded our present position.

I estimated a minute had passed since the first shot and I could not hear any orders from Swanny.

"We got to di di mau[38], man." I heard myself yell. "Back the way we came. That's the safest place."

"No way! We can take these guys!" I couldn't tell who had the gung ho voice. I tried to offset him until Swanny could decide what to do.

I reiterated my case. "Not here; not now. They picked this spot for some reason. Charlie ain't stupid. He didn't stumble on us."

Some of us were returning fire. I suppose that was necessary but I did not like to reveal to Charlie as much as he had revealed to us. And then I thought he might be much stronger than the three or four who had fired, just too lure us in; just like the gung ho voice wanted to do.

Rising above the cacophony of our strategic suggestions, I heard an inspired curse. We all heard it and were silent for an instant. Then Swanny spoke clearly, saying, "One of those motherfuckers stung me!"

"How bad!" I asked from my blind prone position.

"Well it ain't fuckin' good," he answered. His volume suggested he was still strong.

Dan-Boy said he was near and would check it out. Our return fire picked up. Dan-Boy called out that Swanny could be moved and asked for someone to help. Donny said he was there.

Finally Donevan called out, "We're moving back; back the way we came. Get back 200 meters." He was in command now.

"Not yet!" I answered immediately. "Let me shift their fire. Give me thirty seconds and then pull out!" I was

---

[38] GI argot for "leave fast."

second in the column. Ralph was point. I called to him, "Ralph, Louie, Ralphy."

"Yeah," he finally answered.

"You and me, brother! We're going ahead 50 meters and fire from there. Make 'em think we're going forward."

"Roger. Wilco."[39]

"You'll cease firing in twenty seconds and pull out, Ralphy. You hear this Dan-Boy?"

Dan-Boy's voice came back firm and clear. "I'll call for the cease fire. Get them off our ass. It's raining lead over here."

I jumped up into a crouch and ran over to the sound I heard from Ralph. He was flat on his belly and not looking up. I slapped him on the head as I went by. He jumped up behind me. We ran through the open brush. There was no protection from bullets, but there was enough cover to hide us.

Dan-Boy called out "Cease fire!" a couple times. And then "Move the fuck out!"

I flopped to the ground behind a small rise in the ground. Ralph fell in beside me and I pushed him away. We wouldn't want one grenade to take us both out.

Someone else was hit. With our cease fire, his cries for help were clearer. He was not as hearty as Swanny. There was no time to speculate on who it might be.

"You see them?" asked Ralph.

I could hear the attack but could not see anything. Then suddenly I saw a rifleflash.

---

[39] Radio jargon commonly inserted into GI-speak. "Wilco" means "will comply"

"I'm your 12, Ralph. Charlie's at 2 o'clock." And I started firing; short bursts; three at a time. Only the first one is aimed because the rifle moves in recoil, but the next two are near where it was first aimed. I went to a new spot and fired a few more bursts. Then I went back to my first place and fired the rest of the magazine.

"Shit, Skinny. I see flashes at 11 o'clock."

""I'll get it," I answered. He would be shooting through me to get at 11 o'clock. I had to move to get any shot in the new direction. It was looking like they had reserves.

I went through three clips. It could not have taken more than two minutes although time was running very fast and it felt like an hour.

"Let's go now!" Ralph called. His voice quavered ominously.

"Two more clips," I answered. Donny needs more space. We got wounded."

"They're moving in. We gotta go!" he called back. He was not firing any more.

"OK. Move out. I'm right behind you," but I knew I had to get through two more clips first. Ralph was distracting me more than helping. I moved and sent a couple bursts, and moved again.

Ralph had gotten scared and thereby become ineffective. He claimed he saw them getting closer. I did not believe him but it was worth a moment's reflection to see if there was any evidence about that. I listened to the incoming fire. It was becoming a familiar sound, especially since we had stopped returning fire. Was it any louder than when I first heard it? I peeked over the rise. A couple flashes at the 2:00 position were visible. I turned to 11:00

and saw someone advance; not close, but closer than before, obviously. And planning to keep coming. Then a second figure moved toward me while the first one provided covering fire; just like we would do.

The guys called me "Skinny-Quick," but these VC were skinnier than me, apparent even with their loose clothes. I figured they were VC, not NVA, because of their clothes although I did not expect VC to be attacking with formal infantry tactics. Maybe they had learned them from us. I watched to see if there were only the two approaching. My range of view was not good enough to be sure and I was not going to stand up any higher. They were probably just boys, not much different than me in that respect. I did not want to hurt them. I had only been firing in their general direction.

One of them advanced again. I did not duck immediately; a quick motion would be easier to spot. I slid down and loaded a grenade.[40] Maybe some extra noise would slow them down from hurting me. I sent them a Willie Peter,[41] hoping it would start a fire and make some smoke and make them think we were standing our ground. A straight smoker would let them know we were leaving, assuming they knew our usual tactics. Right away, I fired off a frag to make a boom. If they knew our arsenal, they would recognize it as the killer. I fired it at the figures I had seen. They were probably within range now but it was not likely the round would be close enough to harm them. Two grenades counted for one full clip in my accounting. I

---

[40] The grenade is loaded into an "over-and-under," a combination M-16 and grenade launcher.

[41] Slang for "WP," referring to a white phosphorus grenade.

finished off the magazine in my rifle and put in a fresh one before heading back to the squad. I was in low brush and tall grass, not hard to see but I zigged and zagged to be hard to hit. I listened to see if the pops were coming any faster with me in view but did not notice any change. In ten or twenty seconds, I was away from them.

I headed down into a swale where I could not be seen by the VC. Two hundred yards back, Donny had said. That would be about thirty seconds of scrambling, I guessed. I dropped to one knee and listened. All was silent: no shooting, no shouting, no screams of pain, no mortar fire, no whisper of "the squad is assembling over here." Of course I did not recognize anything. I had been paying attention to the route we walked before the attack, but there were no near landmarks. I thought of where a likely rally point might be from the last hour or so. One thing I knew: the squad would not leave me. With two casualties, they would have to move slowly. This was not over and the VC would know that.

A few shots broke out and then a few more. The pattern made me suspect it was the pair advancing. If so, they were helping orient me. I made a guess where our route had been. With the VC still firing, I could move away from them at the same time. I turned to left and right to find a familiar scene. A minute or two went by. I fired off another frag toward the shooting at an angle to maximize the distance from me. I ran quickly for a hundred yards more and knelt down to listen. Mostly I heard myself panting.

I was near a fair-sized tree and I slid up along the trunk to see farther away from my full height. I saw a VC squatting on his heels and looking off at an angle to me. He did not know where I was, although he might have been looking at the rest of the squad. He was within range. I could hit him. I took aim. Leaning against the tree, I was steady. He was too far off to see as an individual but I imagined I saw his smooth, young profile; his underfed, rangy body; his ill-equipped weaponry; his short, lonely, pain-filled future. If I fired over his head, I would give away my position. If I fired at him, I might hold off an attack on the squad, but that was very unlikely. I dropped my aim and scrambled away another hundred yards.

I found a low place where I felt safe resting for a few moments. I felt the irony that I would seek high ground to get oriented if I were lost in the woods, but here I was as lost as I had ever been and I was seeking to reduce the horizon's distance.

There was a rustling not far off. I doubted Charlie would be so loud so I went toward it, quick and quiet. Soon I recognized a dense flurry of obscenity, a beautiful sound at that moment.

"I'm coming in!" I called out moderately loudly so they would not do Charlie's job for him and rejoined the squad, that is, I caught up with the rear guard of the squad. Donny was calling in artillery. With my arrival, he told them to fire one round. A smoke popped up a few seconds later.

"What do you think, Skinny?" Donny asked. "You saw 'em last."

"Which direction is the battery?" I asked. The round was safely beyond us. A small miss would not take us out. "Good." I said. "Do it now."

Donny spoke into the radio, "Fire for effect." And then we moved away as the barrage began. Technology trumped local knowledge of the terrain.

XXXI: Ambush

We did a few night ambushes. Nothing ever happened, nothing that we knew about anyway. We saw less at night so we could always guess someone heard us coming or watched us set up and warned off an NVA patrol. We liked to think something like that happened and that we had at least disturbed someone's plan for the night. Coming back was hard in the dark. I preferred to stay out all night so we would not run into anything: booby trap or VC patrol.

Except the one time. It felt like the others at first. I was even getting used to them, maybe preferring night ambush because we saw less. It had been planned by someone else. Before we went out, Swanny read us the order. Swanny had re-uped for another tour in the Nam. I never asked him why. He would know nothing he could say about it would make any sense to me. I believed he stuck with what he knew. He was appreciated here more than in the world.

Our order sounded like others we had heard. In fact, it was so much like the others, we figured they were all just the same text with new coordinates. We did not recognize the coordinates of the location so the orders did not mean much to us. There was presumably a reason for the coordinates. We never knew what the reason was but it was suggested that there was intelligence intimating the right place for an ambush. Units of two or three at a time carrying supplies. We would just as soon not have a good reason for an ambush, just as soon go through the motions of walking through the bush loaded with our gear, taking our risks, getting sweaty from the heat and humidity until it rained on us and then being cold in our wet clothes, scratched by the brush, eaten by mosquitos, stiff from avoiding movement, until it was time to hike back.

We left in the late afternoon and went to the first location coded into our orders. We waited there for dark. We were supposed to be alert while we waited but some of the guys got relaxed from doing too many ambushes. They were safer than recon[42] or S&D[43] patrols since we did not move around as much, did not expose ourselves to booby traps as much. It was macho to be casual as long as it only affected your own safety. It always affected everyone's safety to be casual but we were all play-acting too much to accept the danger that had been described in our training. It was too much to be fearful all the time. And ambushes were better than other treks in the field because they did not require us to hump[44] as much. We were not out as long so we did not need as much water or food (water being the heavier part).

We did not even have an M-60[45] with us on this ambush. It was usually a comfort to have that hardware but it was a lot to hump, especially with the ammo, and, as the biggest member of the squad, I would have been the one humping it. On the whole, I expected no action and was glad we were going light.

The ambush would be a classic ell formation. We would line up most of us along the trail and have a few in another line at right angles to the trail. The crossing line

---

[42] Reconnaissance

[43] Search and destroy

[44] Carry

[45] A machine gun weighing 23 pounds that could be fired from the shoulder but was usually a two-man weapon fired from a bi-pod.

could not get into positon until we knew which direction our target would be moving. The ell puts fire on the target from two directions without placing us in front of our own guns.

We left our resting point by the clock, when Swanny said there was just the right amount of time to move into positon before it got too dark to see what we were doing. We hiked a couple clicks through second growth forest to a small knoll. It was easy walking with little undergrowth, but too scrubby to be called "parklike." We saw no trails or agriculture or villagers. There was nothing deserving of the name "jungle" although I was still looking for something like that. We crossed something dense enough for the term, but it was just a narrow patch in one of the steep valleys.

The trees had been cut down in this area, probably to make charcoal. That work would have been done several years before we passed and I saw no specific sign of it. Of course, I was not looking to read the natural history of the landscape as I would back in Connecticut. Rather, I was always looking for signs of booby traps or, less likely, ambush against us. Setting up an ambush reminds you they can do the same thing. It was pleasant enough to walk through the forest but I would not for a moment confuse it with tourism.

The knoll was our rally point. If things went badly and we had to scramble, this is where we would meet. This is where the chopper would find us for dust-off[46] or medivac.[47] I had never needed the rally point although I had

---

[46] Helicopter extraction
[47] Medical evacuation

been on a few hawk missions[48] by now, too many to be sure just how many since I did not notch my rifle butt or anything else. Some guys kept track of their missions.   No one counted their kills; there were too few to need to count them and hardly ever did we know if we killed someone anyway. We just shot at somebody or something sometimes or answered fire coming from some invisible source. We were 11-B, small arms infantry; small arms were not the way to kill people in Vietnam. In the modern era, things were very wrong if your rifle was all that stood between you and the enemy.

I did not know what signs Swanny was looking for to set up the ambush. I could be a help but it was not Swanny's way to ask anyone's advice. I did not trust Swanny entirely; he was no genius, but he was the sergeant and he had earned his rocker[49] so I accepted my chances with him. What alternative did I have? ...Probably only to engage with him and give my unwelcome two cents worth. Swanny thought I was smart and he liked me, but he may have liked me more for respecting his opinion or his rank, he would not know or care which, than for being smart. He may not have thought I was smarter than him, just more educated. I was an educational failure among the people I knew before being nearly drafted. In the land of the blind... I suspected he was at least as smart as me in terms of natural brain power. I had the advantage of educational opportunity, if

----

[48] Hawk missions were usually a few days away from base camp followed by an equivalent amount of time back at the base.
[49] The insignia of a buck sergeant in made of three stripes pointed upwards, called "chevrons." The next step up has three chevrons and an arced stripe underneath, called a rocker.

not accomplishment. We had ended up in the same place, both against our will I now knew. Swanny had graduated from high school and gone to work in a hardware store in a small town in South Dakota. He had built up a general knowledge of machinery. He could, he assured me, fix anything on a lawnmower. He was unmarried and had never had a girlfriend but, he assured me, he had found a good prospect until the night he hit a pedestrian with his car. I knew Swanny was a boozer so I assumed he had too much to drink that night but he never said why he had the accident. And he never said how badly he hurt the guy. He did tell me the judge offered him a choice between jail and enlisting.

So neither one of us was bright enough to keep himself out of a situation so absurd I could not believe it existed when I sat back and examined it even though I was looking without benefit of booze, pot, or horse. Maybe that is why I was such a mellow participant in the war; why I would follow a Swanny off any reliable map into a territory known to harbor people bent on killing me and apparently skilled at their business. I did not believe in my core that it was real, at least I did not believe it for a while, just as I did not believe I could possibly be kicked out of school. In the field, we all thought about why were there, why we were not too scared to be there. None of us lacked the appearance of courage; any of us would have gone where we were told to go, but it may have been some of us just did not comprehend the reality of it. At times, I think now I might just have been too lazy to object. Neither of those is courage. Odd that the weakness that got me to the war was the one that made it bearable.

The light was still good when we settled into position. There was a trail near a small stream. That was all I saw of the target zone. We had been in relatively uniform second growth forest for the last click, and walking through flat land since leaving the rally point. There had not been much to mark our route so I wondered if I would have any trouble retracing it if I had to. I thought I would find my way, I usually did. But I doubted all the city kids in the squad could do it on their own. Most of them could not really read a map despite our training and most of them did not pay much attention to where were walking, being focused on VC, booby traps, or dreams.

The largest trees were two or three inches thick, possibly two or three years' growth. They were not especially close-spaced, for reasons I could not understand, so there was enough light reaching through them to support heavy undergrowth. Fortunately, it was not thorny. It made good cover. We could not be seen from thirty feet away, and, of course, could not see anyone thirty feet away from us. Ten yards is not far to be from someone who would wish you dead and has the capability to make his wish come true. It was also good territory for showing where anyone had recently passed. We could be tracked, I supposed, although I had never heard of VC tracking a U.S. patrol. There were plenty of possible perils I had not heard in our training or in the GI bullshit.

Swanny had gone ahead and then come back to explain where the trail was. He said his information was that Charlie was traveling in small groups, two or three at a time, to the south, that is, from our left to our right. Reportedly they were transporting arms to their units farther south although the rational for our ambush was of no interest to any of us in the squad. He took Dan-Boy with him to set out the Claymores. I was surprised he had not tasked me; I was usually his second. Maybe he had in mind that I would keep the rest of the squad quiet and together while he went out; maybe he did not give me a thought. He came down the line and showed each of us our field of fire and whispered the usual warning: wait until the Claymores went off before opening fire. They would blow when Charlie tripped one of the tripwires or Swanny squeezed the clicker. Then shoot like hell until he calls it off. If circumstances demanded, we would fire at own our own initiative. He did not need to remind us of the rest of the drill. We would search the victims for intelligence and then move off to the rally point. I always doubted there would be any intelligence to find unless it were something subtle, in which case none of us would be sophisticated enough to see its value anyway. And here again came that rationalization that someone with the power to make this war occur must be far beyond me in understanding how the world works.

At my immediate level, I recognized the unease of being near a bunch of armed Claymores. The mines looked like cheap, green, plastic stereo speakers, but I had seen them fire and been told countless times of their potency so I respected them despite their appearance. They were indiscriminant weapons, scattering chaos over a wide, if not deep, area. It took significant faith in Swanny and Dan-Boy to hold my position while they set up the ambush and held the clicker that could fire them. There was not much objective reason for faith in either man. At this point, I had lost the habit of concern over risk and simply lay on my chest and elbows, watching any movements by Swanny and

Dan-Boy that I could see. I could not get a strong sense of where the trail lay that they were booby trapping.

I had a nice soft place in the leaves to await the dark. The day's hike had not been overly strenuous, although I was tense with the possibility of ambush coming up. There was a comfortable layer of sweat in my clothes, not so much I would be cold when the sun was gone. I had laid my water and extra ammo beside me and I reached out to feel them from time to time. Everything else remained strapped on me. I sat the water down because it was heavy and I could leave it behind if I had to scramble. The ammo was where I could reach it to reload. It was a familiar exercise. I thought little about what I was doing, saving my attention for the sounds of the forest, for something unusual among them. It would be highly unusual to actually find any VC.

Close to the equator, the sun sets near six o'clock throughout the year and the dusk is short. Any night in our part of Vietnam, especially a dry, moonless night without clouds, was darker than any night I remember in the States. Being out in the bush at night was a really bad idea and that is exactly why they were more likely to travel on moonless nights and why we were holding our ambush now. Anyone who would pass by this spot at night must deserve to die, right? We were not going to see them well enough to analyze their nationality, politics, occupation, gender, or age.

Swanny came by again. "You're on the flank," he whispered with his hand pressed into my back almost intimately. "Hold your fuckin' fire." Then he was gone. What he meant, and he knew I understood, was that I would be the first one to see anyone coming along the trail. I should not get too excited; I should wait for him to reach the tripwire. Swanny knew I was cool-headed. Swanny knew everyone else would see him after me, if anyone actually came along before daybreak, and they would find confidence in my silence up to the point when the Claymores went off. They would have confidence that I was awake and that I would be sure no one escaped out the back in the unlikely event they survived the first blast and the rain of rifle fire right afterwards. Waiting to the right moment to fire was also important so we would not warn anyone coming along after the first person. Large groups of VC kept a point man well ahead of the main body, or so we had been told.

My comfort lasted about thirty minutes. Then my elbows were getting noticeably sore. I did not want to sit up where I might be seen in the waning light but even more, I did not want to be paralyzed by cramps in my joints. I flexed my arms one at a time, slowly, silently. I was proud that I was so quiet but even more proud of the squad that I did not hear a thing from any of them. In a pinch, they were a good bunch; I could count on them as much as anyone I had known in civilian life; count on them to do their job, to be serious when they needed to be, but, more extraordinary, to stand behind me no matter what; no matter what; no matter what.

Another thirty minutes and it was about as dark as it could get. I could see stars through the thin tree cover above; nothing at all at ground level. My aching joints were not unbearable; youth has many advantages. I moved one limb after another, always returning to something like my original stance but shifting the weight around slowly and surviving without feeling sorry for myself. Staving off cramps was not much of a diversion. Like most of Army life, the whole affair had become deadly boring.

An hour after dark, I took a tropical chocolate bar out of a pouch on my belt. I broke off a bite; it tasted so good, I felt fortunate to be just where I was. Against protocol, I whispered to Dan-Boy. It only seemed right that I should offer some to him. He whispered back from somewhere closer than I expected. He shuffled himself over beside me and I gave him half the chocolate bar. He did not say "thanks." No need. He ate his part slowly and then without any further word, shuffled back to his position. We were as close as soldiers are in the field.

Part of a moon rose. Only a third of the moon was lit. It was enough light to see a confusion of grey and white vegetation. With my eyes a foot or so above ground level, my mind saw a dense jungle. Being aware of the environment is a legitimate use of time and energy while in ambush, so I craned my neck to see the moon. It was only a bright area behind some thin clouds. I was nearly sitting up to see it when I heard the sound of water, that is, of something in the water off to my left. I lowered myself slowly and carefully. The sound was dim but I heard it again and again, getting louder. It could only be something walking in the stream. A clash of rocks punctuated the splashes. Whoever it was walked without great caution. There must have been more than one person or a four-legged animal walking in the stream because I could not make out a break between each step. And then the sound ended, still to my left. If he or they were on the trail, they would pass in front of me in a moment and then hit the tripwire less than thirty seconds after that. My breath came heavy and I opened my mouth to keep myself silent. I was sure Dan-Boy had heard the splashing, maybe others too, down the line. And then I saw him; no details, only the motion of him. He came much too close, ten meters away. Right behind him was another but, more worrisome, I heard the water splashing again. The tripwire would be starting the ambush while an unknown number of VC, people anyway, were still approaching. Unknown number of enemy. I wanted to get to Swanny to tell him to disarm the Claymores. I could not get to him in time and I could not get to him quietly. I flipped off the safety. I would lay down fire at the ones still coming. When it began, I would call out to Dan-Boy to fire that way too. I saw the legs of the second person go by, also much too close. I began a countdown to thirty seconds from when the first person passed...

I was shaking as if I were, and maybe I was, cold; could not say. I did not notice any fear; I was focused hard on the trail; I knew now exactly where it went by me and it was much too close. The splashing continued. Thirty seconds was taking a very long time. These VC were in for it; for a terrible surprise. We were in for it too, more than we bargained for. We expected overwhelming advantage but I was doubting it was like that this time. Why had it happened to me? It was not just luck that got me to Vietnam but it was not much else that got me to this ambush; luck and trusting the intelligence reports and analysis of people who knew far more than me about the situation and far less than I needed to know.

My countdown ended without incident. I knew I had not counted too fast. Swanny must have disarmed the Claymores somehow. Were the guys assigned to the short line of the ell, the ones firing along the trail able to hide themselves? I saw another pair of legs pass, and then another. They were all I could see of the enemy and I thought I ought to be gathering intelligence. This was my first encounter this close, closer than the poor abstract sapper I had shot so long ago in the wires at Cha Rang. I had been shot at from a distance and fired at distant shapes in free fire zones. I had walked past booby traps designed to harm me but, as far as I knew, I had no effect on any particular enemy soldier since the Cha Rang incident just as none had any direct effect on me. I should note details of their uniforms, if they were wearing uniforms. I should identify what weapons they were carrying. It was too dark and too obscured to say. More came. I counted them. When ten had gone by I realized our squad was outnumbered. When another ten had gone by I knew I was unable to keep a good count. My dad would have said "Just count the legs and divide by two." More than one was passing at a time and some were too far for me to see them through the brush. Finally the splashing stopped. And then, finally, no more legs went by. Their numbers were unknown exactly, but I guessed twenty five to thirty VC had gone by. I checked my tremors; I was shaking uncontrollably, almost audibly. I counted another 30 seconds and then another. No sound. I called to Dan-Boy. He came over to me. "What was that?" he asked, his lips nearly pressed against my ear, his steel pot[50] tapping against mine. "Did you see anything?"

I answered "Fuckin' A. I count 25, maybe more."

"Twenty five what? What did you see?"

"VC, man. They had to be VC."

"Twenty five? Where'd they go?"

---

[50] Helmet.

"Left to right, up the trail."

"No way. No one went past me."

"Pass it down to Swanny. Twenty five VC went by. We got to di di mou."

A long minute later Swanny came up on me and asked what I had seen and I told him. So he took me out to the trail. We could see the column had turned just where they were closest to me, turned away from our ambush, saving themselves and saving us. They had not really used the trail. They came down the small streambed and then crossed the trail and went off in an unmarked direction, unmarked as far as we could tell in the dark. Swanny and I were as quiet as we could be. We stayed close to each other and whispered what we could see. I expected him to yell "bug out" at any moment and we would all head out for the rally point on our own. I hoped it did not come to that. In the dark, someone would be lost for sure. The tension was greater every moment we stayed. More might be coming or the ones that went by might come back or might hear us from wherever they were now.

"We can't follow," Swanny said.

I did not answer any more than an affirmative grunt, although I had an urge to ridicule his statement. Of course we could not follow them. I took his comment as a way of saying we had done the best we could. A serious soldier like Swanny would regret making no more of a rare opportunity like this to engage the enemy. My faith in him was rewarded by his accepting we would have very little to show for the incident tonight. Some gung-ho mothe's would have gotten all John Wayne and tried something more. Anything more would have been damn foolish. Swanny gathered us together and briefed us again on where the rally point was and then led us together back to it. I was still shaking when we got there and settled in for the rest of the night, but not so much anyone could see it in me. The shaking bothered me like a cancer yet I had no thought of abandoning my responsibility, my post, my squad. No one would have said anything if they had seen my shivering.

Poem for Myself
Don't care 'bout the rise of the Reds;
Don't care 'bout the steel pots on our heads;
Don't care 'bout the rain or the heat;
Don't care 'bout the miles on my feet;
Don't care 'bout the bugs in my bed;
Don't care 'bout the nameless dead.
Don't care 'bout how to brag;
Don't care 'bout the American flag:
I care about keepin' my body intact,
And about the rude GI who's got my back.

XXXII: Issac

Isaac was the only one in our squad who showed concern for our risks. The rest of us outwardly adopted the fatalism of soldiers in every time and place. I admired his fear, his humanity, his intellectualism. I fit in much too comfortably with the other grunts around me. It was right to respect them, but I should have aspired to a higher station. Isaac was in the lower end of the class to which I had been born and he was a fine example of the class I needed to rise toward as an adult.

We all respected Isaac and that is why we did not resent his skipping out on the field, respect for his abilities and also a widespread discomfort with beating the bush alongside him. In the bush he was the weak link. He was unintentionally noisy, sloppy in his packing, clumsy in walking, boring in conversation, unreliable in aiming his rifle, inattentive to the signs of the forest, slow in the pace of his march, and he snored uncontrollably at night.

Isaac did not allow himself to be the pawn in this game, although that was his rank, like ours. He talked the manager of the PX into letting him apply his accounting skills to their vulnerabilities. An audit would be coming up someday and Isaac was far better qualified than anyone in the PX system to clean up the books. The PX manager tried him out and apparently was impressed so he used his considerable influence to get Isaac assigned to help out. But the assignment was temporary and somehow informal. I did not understand it. Isaac remained in our hooch and came to our formations but he would disappear after chow and the CO formed our hawk teams without him.

Isaac, Dan-Boy and I were coming due for R&R. The Colonel above us, whom I never saw through my entire tour, put a notice on the board one day to say the unit was short staffed. So he said although everyone would get an R&R, the order of going would be based on how many days we had spent in the field rather than simply how many days we had been in-country. This order was received enthusiastically by us grunts because it showed respect for the risks we faced. Only the three of us were actually eligible for R&R when the notice came out, but the whole company was pleased about it. Until we noticed it would delay Isaac. You never know if the Army will keep its promises. If Isaac missed his time now, he might never get the R&R. So our top[51] worked out a plan for me to work in the PX for a week and while Isaac went to the bush for a week to get his numbers up. There were so many purely support personnel, one more week in the bush would be enough to get Isaac on a plane to the fantasy of his choice.

I went to the prep meeting for the next trek. It was a search-and-destroy. They were checking on a possible bunker complex. Probably it was an old one abandoned before the French had left Vietnam, but it needed to be removed from the map. I was surprised that I really did stay back this time. I filed things for the PX manager for a week. It was a much better job than my usual one despite its boredom. I would willingly be bored for a year to ensure all my limbs stayed attached.

Isaac lost no limbs on his mission, but he lost a lot of his blood. The bunkers were crumbling and unoccupied, which was not the whole story since there was a firefight on the way back. Isaac took three rounds. That was very unusual. The first round usually brings you down where you are a poor target. Isaac was in the open and was hit again over several minutes before the guys routed Charlie and moved Isaac off to a chopper. We went over to the hospital in the evening to see him but we were too late. I never got to say "goodby." He never got his R&R.

XXXIII: R&R

At six months into my tour, June, halfway to DROS, it was all routine, not boring, but familiar. There was an

---

[51] Slang for the highest ranking sergeant in the company.

ease in our way of life, for which we paid by living the risks of a base in disputed territory and by occasional forays into the bush. It was assumed that anyone who spent the full tour with regular runs in the bush would get hit with something.

Once settled into the life, it was not hard to take. Our work when at the base was not demanding for the most part: guard duty, KP, cleaning up equipment, and such. We had steaks for dinner, softball in the afternoon, drinking and gambling at night and some girls to tease at the club or smoking weed in the hooch with the music of the day to console us. There was no concern over clothing, fashion or hair styles. No one's mother or father demanded that he study harder or bring in a bigger paycheck. Sex was available without any pressure to be attractive oneself at the massage parlor on base more or less legally, or in the local vil more excitingly. We did not even have to salute the officers. It was considered a tip-off to snipers about who was the more important target. We regularly had free entertainment from Asian or Australian troupes, cheap goods from the PX, no living expenses, warm weather, and a week of R&R after six months. R&R was even better than being on the base. All the amenities were in abundance and the risky job was put aside.

The grunts I knew whiled away many long hours in the club nursing a succession of beers to help them discuss how to do R&R. The topic was studied with an intensity most of us had never applied to anything in our military or civilian lives. Those who had already gone loved to relive, embellish, and boast of their adventure and those who had not yet gone wanted to dream all the completed ones and plan their own optimal version. For most of us, R&R

offered a fantasy we had never expected to experience, beyond any promise made by recruiters, regardless of who was doing the dreaming.

If you wanted sex, supplemented by companionship, Thailand was the best option. A mama-san would be waiting at the bottom of the airplane steps to take you to her establishment where you would select your girl for the week. She would show you the sights, take you to dinners and teach more than any of us knew before about sex. The girls came with a guarantee. If you did not like her for any reason, you could turn her in.

Hong Kong offered some of the same but its specialty was cheap prices on any object. Hand-made suits were often mentioned.

Australia offered the same kind of companionship but with white women although that is not how they were characterized by GIs; they were called "round-eyes." White GIs who came back from there thought they were in love and wrote faithfully back to the girls who had kept them company although I never heard the claim in any of the stories told at the club that any of these girls ever wrote back.

When it was my turn to design a week in heaven, I could not visualize myself in a brothel. I suspected I liked sex as much as the next guy but I feared gonorrhea more than the VC. At least injury or death from the designated enemy of America was respectable to someone, my parents for example. Everyone thought getting a sexually transmitted disease was disreputable, everyone except the Army and nearly everyone who had already taken R&R and spoke of it in my presence. I did not lack the nerve, I thought, to engage an R&R prostitute, but it was a different kind of challenge from facing the VC. Having come to the war, I had agreed to take my chances with the VC. The decision was made; the results would come out wherever they came out. I did not revisit the decision. R&R was a reward, deservedly or not, and it was no place to add to the contradictions of my self-image and moral burdens of my time overseas.

But if I had given full rein to my id, I would have gone to Thailand to play out my passions for Mai. It would have been disloyal to imagine intimacy with anyone else even if the intimacy were in fact practiced with someone else. A Thai girl would remind me of Mai more than an Australian or Chinese one, or so I imagined.

I might have arranged for an R&R with a buddy if one were coming due for his own. Dan-Boy was the only person I knew who might have shared my interests, but our talks about R&R revealed we did not have as much in common as I had thought. He seemed to feel it was our responsibility to do something thoroughly irresponsible to legitimate our whole overseas experience. He came across as having more guts than me since I was apparently afraid of getting a bug that a shot of penicillin could cure easily enough. He was so aware of doing what was expected of him that it extended to having a rowdy time he did not actually want. How did I know I would feel miserable in the morning, so miserable the evening was not worth it, if I never got drunk? How would I know I had cheapened Mai or women more generally by paying for a faux relationship if I had never tried it? Where is the harm? Mai was not only not my wife, she was not even my girlfriend. I asked why he did not use that logic to justify trying weed and he was offended by my suggestion. Weed was a stepping stone to drugs, not always, but possibly. And weed was bad for the

167

body, worse than beer, even when the beer was in excess from time to time. Just look at the potheads! They tended to be a bunch of skinny (no offense), pretentious talkers. His cultural roots shown through and they shed light on mine. I belonged with the potheads. I lacked all self-discipline, but I was skeptical of authority and thoughtful, as demonstrated by my constant sense of guilt which I deserved for that lack of self-discipline which allowed the contradictions between what I thought I ought to do and what I did. Besides, it felt a little creepy for someone like myself raised in the plastic suburbs to indulge in the private act of R&R with a buddy. If I were to do things I would not want to admit to the people I would get to know back in the world, better to do them alone.

In a stroke of genius, I filled in the R&R request for a trip to New Guinea. I would see a unique part of the natural world and have an enviable story to tell to the people I expected to know someday without any odor of debauchery. The company clerk laughed and tore up my application. "Just the R&R posts and why the fuck would you ever want to go to New Guinea?" I felt like I was buying a skin mag in the drug store across the street from the family church.

Thailand? A week of pretending Mai was reachable? Australia was too much like home; not seeing the world. I filled in "Hong Kong." I would see nothing of nature. I had no use for a suit. I did not like Chinese food. The only thing I wanted to buy was a car and that needed to wait until I was back in the States. Its reputation had a patina of sleaze that would allow others to assume for my time whatever decadence they would have wished for themselves and, at that moment, standing before the company clerk's unstable wooden table, I was not sure whether I would not accept some of the depravity on offer. Dan-Boy had made a good case in some ways.

The momentum of my life carried me through R&R without changing me, except for the laudable lesson that I did like Chinese food. On the first day, I rose early and walked the streets outside my hotel sopping up the chaotic colors and sounds and smells of the open markets. It was exciting to be someplace so exotic, building Asian memories to offset the muddy filth of my war. Everyone knew by my age and haircut that I was a GI but I did not feel targeted by my obvious reason for being there, not during the daylight.

By ten am, feeling happily free, I adopted a purpose: to try some Chinese food. I said I did not like Chinese food; it was like the way I did not like Indian curry or German stews. I could not remember ever trying any of these. The roast duck hanging in restaurant windows looked very appetizing. Rice was always nice. I went into a small place, one that looked more like a New England diner than a foreign restaurant. The menu had no English. The waitress was older than my mother and she spoke no English. I had taken Spanish in high school but had not learned much and doubted it would have helped at all. I pointed to the duck in the window. She smiled and was satisfied that I had ordered clearly. She brought green tea and proffered sugar in cubes which I pushed off in my sophistication. She brought a dish of mixed vegetables that I could mostly identify so I ate them with confidence. She showed me how to use chopsticks although I refused to hold the bowl next to my face and push food in as she suggested. I was not ready to go that local. Before I finished the vegetables she brought the dish of duck. It was sliced, not like the ones hanging in the window but much more manageable for that since I had no knife. And the rice was sticky enough to eat with chop sticks so I felt pretty good about myself when I finished my first Chinese meal. After that, I ventured a step further from the familiar whenever I ate but not all the way into the realm of eating peculiar animals being fried in the stalls in the street.

In that first day, at Hong Kong's low prices, I bought expensive sunglasses that folded into a small case, and a self-winding watch from Korea. After seeing their soldiers, I had particular respect for Koreans. I decided to buy one thing each day after that and to stick to things small enough to carry back to the LZ, rather than store something at HQ.

Over the week, I took a boat tour of the harbor, watched a movie, wandered through the zoo, read a book of poems (i.e., the poems that caught my fancy in the first few lines), and on the next to last day, went to a strip show. It was fun to shop around for the right one and to know I was about to step across an arbitrary line no one would deny me. The show would have been disappointing if I had hoped for a passionate experience. A succession of girls danced to taped music. They looked good enough and revealed more than I had ever seen on a living female, but there was no sexual thrill to it. I remembered the freak shows on the mid-way at the county fair in the 1950s. I had never gone into one but I knew whatever was inside was a sad imitation of what was being promised. A few boys followed me from the club to see if I wanted further education. It took me two blocks to convince them I was boring, not bored. Feeling mature and powerful, I took a long route back to my hotel.

I was accosted three more times by women, all of whom looked good to me. They took "no" for an answer easily enough. I hoped I communicated assertiveness and that they would appreciate that I did not waste their time by pretending to be interested.

XXXIV: Leading the Mission

Nine months in the Nam. My newbie days were long gone. Nine months in the world was not much time but here it was three fourths of a tour. I was in the habit of counting down daily: 91 days and a wake-up to DROS. I talked to Dan-Boy about my achievement during our morning formation while waiting for the officers to decide what to do with us this day. Since I was in the unit before him, Dan-Boy would need a couple days more to reach the same mark. Our work assignments for the day would be posted, but they made it easier for us by reading them off in the formation. A high percentage of the unit could not read, not read well any way. We were relaxed, used to waiting, knowing we would get our bullshit work details in a few minutes and then be off to chow. It was still cool enough to be comfortable. We still had one more day until we would go out to the field again.

I hadn't noticed that Swanny was missing. When the lieutenant came out and we were called to our half-hearted attention, there was a gap in our pattern, showing his place. We heard our bullshit assignments for the morning and then the Lieutenant ended by saying I should report to the CO[52] after chow. I figured he had some bad news from home for me and I worried through breakfast what it might be but when Dan-Boy asked me why I was seeing the old man, I just shrugged my incomprehension. We did not expect to understand what the Army was doing to us.

The Captain had me sit down after I reported to him with my best salute. He appealed to my ego, a substantial vulnerability for me, and nearly had me but the weight of my nine months of experience with the war kept me from enjoying his announcement. He said Swanny had some kind of bug and would be out for a week or more. He was taking Swanny's recommendation that I fill in for him on our next hawk mission. I knew Swanny was getting real short[53] and suspected he was finished with the field. A few weeks earlier I had advanced from PFC[54] to Spec 4[55], and the CO said I could act as an E-5 for one mission when the company was short-handed. He muttered conspiratorially that neither he nor I would want a shake-and-bake[56] to take us out. He asked if I were up to the task. I answered too quickly. Yes, of course I was up to the task in the sense of being able to do it. He asked how many missions I had done in the field. I told him I did not know but that I was down to 91 and a wake-up (that's how we enumerated our

---

[52] Commanding Officer. In this case, it was a company formation and the CO would be a Captain.

[53] Close to the end of his tour.

[54] Private First Class, enlisted rank 3.

[55] Specialist at the level of enlisted rank 4. This is equivalent in level to a corporal but the Army no longer had corporals. Corporals had been the lowest rank with command authority.

[56] A buck sergeant who obtained his stripes by going to a school rather than by spending time in rank.

remaining days). He liked that I did not keep count of missions. Doubtless his confidence in me was also influenced by the Bronze Star I received for that stunt in Cha Rang. It should not have figured into his thinking. It was too long ago; that was not me anymore. It was not me even back then.

In my mind, I could take the team out on an assignment as well as most of the E-5s I had met. None of them had much more experience than my nine months or my indeterminate tally of times in the bush. It was only a recon mission this time; search and destroy took no more expertise but was more responsibility. I had my fill of "destroy" with my first encounter back in the wires at Cha Rang. Everything since then was just self-preservation for myself and my squad; like everyone else, just get back home even if in my case and many of those around me, home was not there anymore. We were too old to go back to our parents, too young to have any other home.

I had six on my team, including myself. I knew them all well. There were no newbies among us. I was the shortest, but no one had more than six months to go. No one was going to feel threatened or otherwise object to my being in charge. They were an easy bunch, worn down now by accepting orders for at least a year each. None of them was especially rebellious before getting into the Army. Probably I was the one least likely to accept authority although I was better than most at appearing to be part of the machine.

Ralph would be my second, someone who was smart and careful. We had some long talks back in the hooch or over a beer in the NCO club. We liked the same music. We both liked to hike in the hills back home although we agreed not to look at our hikes in Nam as anything but business. He would have been a scholar if he had half a chance like they say people always get in America. He felt urban to me, probably because of my prejudice against the brain power of rural people. He was from Louisiana and had basic at Ft. Polk so we had that place in common for conversation. That was the farthest he had been from his hometown up until then. And the farthest anyone in his family or anyone he knew had ever been from his hometown, including his pastor and his teachers. Of course, going to Vietnam set a new record for travel for him. He said the whole town was proud of him, except for himself. He saw no basis for pride in letting himself be carried to the far side of the earth for purposes completely unknown to himself. We called him "Louie." That was because of the way he pronounced "Louisiana" in a way none of us remembered hearing before but was so beautifully musical, we had it in mind whenever we spoke with him.

With Swanny out, Dan-Boy was the only other white guy on the mission. Isaac was not going out with us obviously, but it still felt as if he should be there. It would be easier without him along but I took no comfort in that. I wondered if anyone else was thinking of it, of his tendency to stumble into things, to drift onto established trails, to make noise with his poorly packed gear, to drag the pace with his breathy efforts. I suspected we all enjoyed taking care of him. It made us feel superior for the moment while knowing he was likely to be the one on top of us all back in the world. He had never shown the least arrogance about that and was always humbled by his need for us, but we all knew he was destined for a material success none of us was likely to see, except, maybe, for Dan-Boy who had connections in the used-car industry and might become a big deal in his part of Georgia.

Neon Leon was a tall, loud fellow from South Carolina. We called him "neon" because he was so country, so square, he would not know what neon lights were. He looked athletic but he was actually soft. His long arms and oversized hands gave him a rangy look I would have preferred in my body to the "skinny" characterization that usually came to mind for me. Maybe the difference was only that he looked more mature despite being a year younger than me.

Looking the part was good enough for him. He had joined up a year after high school. He was going to be drafted anyway but that is not why he joined. He was not getting anywhere in his small town and did not know how to get out except for the Army. It was a common and respected approach to upward mobility in his community. He did not tell me this, but I could hear the respect in his otherwise brash tone for the Green Machine, a respect few others at our level would admit.

He ignored me for the most part. There was nothing disrespectful in it. He did not know anyone like me and did not feel he was missing anything important. He thought I had been privileged and that I did not appreciate it. I could feel it in his distain although he never made the least judgmental comment in my presence, not about me or anything else. I suspected he knew his Bible but the topic never came up. I also thought that he would be the most courageous of any of our group if it ever came to that. He just accepted the world in front of us and did what he thought ought to be done regardless of any analysis of consequences.

Ray was the oldest member of our group at 22 years of age. He had worked as a housepainter since he dropped out of high school. He said he worked for a few different contractors over the years and learned his trade but wanted more excitement, to be part of what was big in the world. He was so insistent on this story, I did not believe it. I thought he was bored by his life and wanted excitement, true enough, but he did not imagine the Army would provide it. He wanted girls and music and drugs. Maybe he knew enough about Vietnam to know it was easy to get drugs, but I think that was just his good luck. I think he enlisted because he had no better idea, if he enlisted at all. I could not see how he kept out of the draft. He said there were so many people signing up from his neighborhood, the draft board did not need him. I did not necessarily believe that story either. We called him "Charles" because Donevan loved Ray Charles and called him that. When Donevan gave someone a name, it stuck because Donevan was cool, cooler than Ray Charles in my opinion because Ray Charles seemed a little too country to me.

Loran, who arrived nearly six months previous and a few days after Ralph, hated his name, and was constantly offering nicknames for himself. They were always poor ideas, based on his vision of a dynamic personality which did not fit him: Atomic, Spike, Tex, Dino... We would try to use them but they were never memorable and they were not advertised well enough that everyone knew them so we always went back to calling him Loran. I tried one out on him, a name that had been used for me briefly in Boy Scout camp. It was adopted for a few days, as successful as any, but ultimately failed, possibly because I was the only one who knew what it meant, although it had the slightly insulting sound of a good nickname: Mumblypeg.[57]   Sure, we called most people by their last names but Loran was "Williams" and so was Ralph so we could not use that for either of them.   The best compromise I could offer was to pronounce only the first syllable of his name with a hint of an "N' afterwards, "Lorn," so it would not be simply "Lore." Which sounded bad by itself.

Loran was broad in the middle for a man of twenty years. Someday he would be fat. This tendency might not fit well with his fascination over women.   When he originated a conversation, he always spoke of them. He had known a few and known them well but it was not the ones he had known that occupied his dreams. He wanted to know others, practically any that he could imagine.   Of course Loran's prospects with women may have been better than I thought. I did not know enough of them to judge what it took. Being fat seemed a liability but it may not have been as significant as I wanted to think. My skinny self wanted to believe women cared a great deal about a partner being firm in body. In the dark, that attribute should have been an asset.

Loran was not dynamic, not especially memorable, but he was a good fellow. Everyone liked him. He told no jokes, showed no distinctive styling, and was not especially conversant in the specialized language of the soul brother, yet his positive attitude was infectious and people liked

---

[57] Mumblypeg is a boy's game in which the players throw a knife in the ground so it sticks as close as possible to his own foot. The closest one wins.

being around him. As far as soldiering went, he was known to be reliable, a much desired attribute in the field. Loran would be where he should be when he should be there. He was not the strongest bearer of equipment, or the best shot, or the most alert, but we were well satisfied with what he brought to the bush.

I went to the company briefing when the rest of my peers went to breakfast and then I grabbed a bite on the run back to the hooch. I showed them the map. It was not ideal. We were used to errors on the map and we were to fix any we found on this trip although we were not really qualified to correct a map unless it was a very clear mistake. We would follow a stream up toward its source, never being actually along the stream where our path would be predictable. Then we were to cross over a low pass into another river basin and continue to a certain mountaintop, avoiding the villages along the way. We would not be predictable but we would not be hidden either.

The villagers do not sit in the village all the time. They will be in the fields and some in the forest and would probably see us before we saw them. We would be stealthy and they would be alert. They had survived in this war longer than any of us.

It was a four-day mission; three nights. We drew LRPs[58] and packed our water and ammo. Everyone took more than the required amount of ammo. Altogether, we had sixty pounds each on us. I went through the checklist on each guy but I did not ask to see everything. They knew their jobs. Mainly I had to be sure we had a weapons

---

[58] Dry, light weight meals for Long Range Patrols.

balance among us. I found nothing to fix and we headed to the chopper pad by 0700.

There were a dozen choppers at the pad and room for more. I read the numbers on their noses and found ours. I showed our orders to the pilot. My ego enjoyed my being the one doing these small things. He had a machine gunner already on board. We took off within minutes, much quicker than any commercial flight would ever be.

I was the last in and sat by the door opposite the gunner. I would be first out. By leaning out the door, I could lose sight of the chopper in my peripheral vision. I was on a flying carpet! The chopper lifted its tail and we spiraled up above the LZ. It was fascinating to see it spread out below us. I knew every construction down there and I knew it was not as clean and dry as it appeared from the bird. I had been up enough times to know we would only get a quick look at the LZ and I concentrated on it, like it was a train set from my childhood. And then we were off. I could orientate in the bush but things moved too fast in the chopper and I could not keep track of our direction unless I looked for the sun and thought about the time of day and then made a general estimate. When I saw the mountains approaching, I got a vague idea of the layout. Besides, I had studied the map so I knew our destination. It was just that we did not go directly to it since we assumed our departures were being watched by the VC.

It was not normally a long trip to the bush since choppers move so fast and we always stayed within the Brigade AO. We dipped down below the height of the bamboo lining the rice paddies and buzzed along a few feet above the water. We really felt the speed of the bird when it flew this low. I did not know why we flew like this. I had ridden this low many times so I supposed it was a policy; maybe to make it harder to track us. The VC had no radar, not in our AO anyway, so anyone tracking us was just watching from somewhere. It was fun for us young guys to ride like this although I wondered if it were being done for the fun and we were taking a risk as we adjusted at the end of each field to rise above the bamboo windbreak. I also wondered if the fun for the pilot was in making the famers drop into the water. I was sure we steered toward them rather than went around them in paddy after paddy.

The pilot turned around and handed me a helmet so I could hear on his intercom. He explained we had to make a detour. Would a fifteen-minute delay harm our mission? Fifteen minutes more in the air only meant to me fifteen minutes less in the bush. He then explained that there was a bombing run in the neighboring AO and he had to keep his distance. We had been told in some class how far away we had to be from any bombing. I did not remember the figure (I did not expect to ever be in a position to choose where to be), but I knew it was a long way off. The air force used 300-pound bombs. Our chopper landed on a barren knoll to wait out the bombing run.

It was hell to be in the vicinity and there was always the possibility that they might drop them in the wrong place. We could see the planes drop their load and a few seconds later, felt the sound blast. It was too far away to seem real to us except that the compression wave took us beyond the sensations possible in a movie theater. I shuddered to think what it must have been like for the people in it and I had no doubt that some of those people did not deserve it, no matter what you thought of the motivations behind the war. We all watched in silence, as if it were a thunderstorm passing by and we each had our own interpretation of what was making the flashes and booms. It did not last long from our perspective. To us, the bombing was just the explosions over a few minutes; less than a Fourth of July fireworks in a small town. To whomever was below those bombs, they were just the start of a new level of pain, if they had survived.

The pilot was on the horn[59] for five minutes after the bombing run. Finally he called us to mount up and we clambered back in the bird, and lifted off. We did not go anywhere nearer the bombing. It was on the other side of the chopper from my window so I never saw the damage. If anyone else saw any more, he did not say anything about it that I heard.

We were dropped off on a dirt road that was marked clearly on the map. As we came in, I looked into the terrain we would recon. The mountains were not high but they were steep and heavily wooded. I hoped for the impression of jungle. So far I had only seen the kind of dense, canopied, viney growth associated with that word in a few small, steep valleys.

The chopper never shut down-- it was on the ground only a few seconds. By the time the thump of his rotors had faded, we were off the road and into some cover. I took a compass bearing and made sure everyone in the squad understood our direction. We checked each other to be sure our gear was complete, secure and quiet. We synced our watches. I assigned Dan-Boy to point for the first leg. I was in the rear where I could keep an eye on things. The first part of our mission was close to a road we controlled and was probably safe. The longer we were out,

---

[59] I.e., the radio.

the less sure we were of our location and the accuracy of the intelligence guiding us. Dan-Boy was feeling fresh and kept a good pace. That was fine with me. I had told him to stop after an hour and knew he would remain aware of the time.

After an hour he did not stop immediately. We had been climbing a narrow ridge and I knew he was looking for better cover. I smiled to think this squad knew what it was doing well enough to run along on its own, at least until a complication turned up. The ridge dipped down and widened toward a small pass. Dan-Boy crouched and everyone stopped. I went up the short column to the front and talked to Dan-Boy. We looked at the map and saw nothing marked nearby. I assigned a separate direction for each of us to watch and we rested for ten minutes. Our shoulders were already burning where the pack straps dug in. A lot of the weight was carried on the utility belt and our clothes bunched up uncomfortably under them and soaked with sweat. It was just the usual hump. No one thought of complaining. No one noticed the discomfort. We were tense with the idea of Charlie.

I looked at my watch as much as the bush in front of me. It seemed important to rest no more than ten minutes. It would be hard to get them moving again if they cooled off too much. When I rose and slung my pack again, I did not need to say anything. A few muttered curses came my way but they were not serious. Besides, they were too low to be heard by Charlie. I took the point for the next leg. I was not moving as fast as Dan-Boy because I was studying the map more than he had. I was looking for something. I had to go outside our planned route to get it and I had not been briefed on the accuracy of the map along its fringes. I was always looking off toward the northeast because I thought that was where it lay. Twice I called a halt and climbed a tree to see farther away. I went up to where the strongest branch remaining could barely hold me and swayed in the breeze. Like most of the guys, I was not scared of falling. I was not in any way superstitious but I was certain that falling from a tree was not how I would escape Vietnam. My hour on the point stretched into 90 minutes and more. No one complained. We were not moving hard. We had not seen any vil up close. Here in the hills, there were only hunters and charcoal makers. And, maybe, VC, but our intelligence did not think so. The hairy places were at least five to ten clicks away, probably more if I understood the way the officer briefing us this morning had tried to exaggerate the danger. I was still waiting for the day when an officer went on one of these hawk missions into the vague parts of the map.

It started to rain before we got to the place I wanted. I had led for two hours without a formal break but my pace and side looks were enough no one felt overburdened. I called for lunch. We kept spread out, took our cover, and faced our personal zone. Fifteen minutes, I told them. They were not used to taking more on such an occasion. I climbed a tree while they were eating their sodden powders and tropical chocolate. We would not have a fire any time in this trip. We were too burdened with the weight of ammo to carry anything in a tin can. After lunch I moved about one more click and told them to set up for the night. It was a little past noon.

Our site was on a rocky outcrop with very steep sides except in one direction. I sent Dan-Boy to guard the way in and gathered the others around me. I told them I did not want to join the Army, did not want to go to

Vietnam and did not want to go on any hawk missions and did not want to be the leader. But all those things fell on me and I just accepted them. Except for the last one. I was not qualified to lead them on a recon mission in the bush, to take on whatever VC and NVA may be around, and to work our way safely through an alien environment, and to return with information that would be useful toward the liberation of the Vietnamese, and we all knew I was not up to the task even if I had been in country for a few months of my twenty years on earth. I took the job because they would only have sent someone worse if I said I would not do it. So I put my proposal up for vote. Whatever we voted, everyone would stick to the decision. We all agreed on my terms. There was a lot of mythology about how young men behave in war and I had seen little idealism among us in the lower ranks, but I was sure this pact would be honored. At least, I was sure it was safe if nothing challenged our account, if there was no crisis or investigation or detailed debriefing. I did not express my reservations about the strength of our pact; they were all enjoying it too much. My proposal was to sit on this rocky outcrop for three days and then go back with about as much intelligence as we would have if we humped our way into the dangerous unknown. I said I could work out a way to have a secret vote using straws or rocks or something. Ralph swore enthusiastically and said there was no need for any secret. No one was going to argue about it and the others all agreed. I sent Ralph up to relieve Dan-Boy so he could have his say and I asked everyone to say nothing until Dan-Boy voted. And Dan-Boy did not ask for a secret ballot when he quietly joined the rest with his vote.

It rained all afternoon and into the night. We rotated guard duty. I took advantage of the rain to explore the vicinity. With the sound of rain and the softness of the wet undergrowth masking my movements, it was a safe time to be moving in the bush. I went as far out as our bodies could be smelled or our snoring heard.

My clothes were wet although it was hard to know whether it was mostly from sweat exuded in a failed effort to cool me, rain that constantly found its way around the edges of my poncho, or drips from the foliage that slapped into my face as I pressed through the undergrowth. Being wet was not a reason for complaint; it was just the way it was. I had no basis for complaint this day. My pain centers were occupied fully by my fear of being caught leading this little mutiny. I felt far braver for confronting my unseen superiors than for going into VC territory. Doing what I was ordered to do was easy; it took no effort, just an acceptance of my impotence. Not going was courageous. Did we not-go out of fear of Charlie? I could not say for the others and I could not say for myself. It just felt like the smarter option now that it was an option. I had made it an option. I had turned the movie logic of youth facing authority into an actual choice. I finally felt like I was part of my generation, those people I had admired in college, the ones who had the courage to stand up to their parents and professors and clergy, the ones who had liberal-minded girlfriends and current styles in clothing and hair and dance. I had the confidence of a leader. I was leading my men, men who did not share my cultural interpretation of the war, led them into a few days of peace, safety and moral integrity. I did not want to discuss these ideas; I did not want to confront the contradictions in my position. The decision was made and we were all committed to living with it.

I struggled to stop my shivering in the steamy heat. The vibrations in my chest revealed the tension I did not consciously feel. I would take a deep breath and feel the shivering stop. A few minutes later I would notice I was shivering again. It was a frustrating sensation, not something expected in a leading man.

It rained all night and my sleep was fitful. It was not the cold wet or the rough ground that bothered me the most; not even the remote but real threat of attack. What bothered me the most was the same form of nightly torture I had experienced camping back in my days of innocence: mosquitoes. Those tiny minions of Satan were, of course, worse in Vietnam because they carried the additional threat of malaria. We took pills but some guys got sick anyway. Even so, I preferred trying to sleep to being on guard. We had two guards up at all times. Their main job was to make sure the other one was awake. Falling asleep on guard duty is so easy, the darkness is so boring— it is hard to appreciate that it is one of the biggest errors someone at our level might make. None of us was prone to the worse offenses like, say, cowardliness in the face of the enemy. I could imagine someone who kept his head down all the way through a fire fight rather than pulled his weight, but I had not seen it and I had not heard of anyone who had seen it first-hand. I had heard of the opposite, of the gung ho warriors who do more than is required. Most of us think they are childish or just suckers.

When the morning came around, I called in a position to headquarters. Not our actual position of course. It was not hard to say where we ought to be. It was only important that nothing came up in our reported location. It also occurred to me that we might be in a world of hurt if they decide on a bombing in our actual location. The odds were in our favor; bombing in our AO was not so common. I wrapped a shirt around the mike when I called so it would sound like we were farther away. The PRC-25 had a range of **3-7** miles but that could vary with terrain and weather. The radio was a big part of our advantage in the field because it allowed us to call in help, offensive or defensive.

Things went bad in an unexpected way. It was a conversation Dan-Boy initiated. He had just come off guard duty and spread his poncho out near me in the sun and lay on it with a log for a pillow.

"Do you think this is your last run in the boonies?

"Do you think this counts as one? Maybe that last trip was the last one. This is just experience showing through."

"This is the boonies. It counts as much as any of 'em. I wouldn't do this for fun. Ain't a one of us would."

"Do you think you have any more trips than me, Dan-Boy?"

"I always figured you were one trip ahead of me."

"We may get outta this place in one piece, Brother."

"I don't think so. Not the both of us."

"I'm gonna grow my hair out when I get back."

"Me too."

"You'll be close to a month behind me. Maybe I'll just wait until you get out too."

"No, man, I'm not a month behind you on getting out of the Machine. I got just 42 days left after DROS."

"No way! Only 42? You'll be out a week before me! You wait a week to start growing your hair?"

"I'd do it but I don't know how. They don't give you a cut on your last day."

"Just try, man."

"I'm gonna get that 20-inch thing."

"Chest to waist?"

"Yeah."

"I couldn't do it, couldn't come remotely close. I tried lifting. It just didn't show up much on me."

"It'll show up on anyone. It takes more work than you might think."

"Yeah, you're probably right. I never stuck with it for long. Truth is, I never worked very hard at anything."

"Think you'll work any harder now?"

"Doubt it. But I wish I would. I guess I was counting on luck and it got me here."

"But it's been good here. Luck is as good a reason as any for deciding who gets back whole."

"Wonder if luck is gonna get me a girl."

"I was thinkin' you'll need to work more to get through school. A girl will turn up. Half the world is girls."

I was feeling down and was admitting my deficiencies. It would have been a good time for Dan-Boy to say I had something more than my dubious luck to look forward to.

"I'll get back to wrestling anyway. I can do that."

"That takes work too, I bet."

"I can work. Maybe I will. I've been putting in calisthenics. I'll be older too. I did not mature as fast as some. Now I've caught up."

Dan-Boy snorted a quiet laugh. "Getting a couple years older will help but not as much as doing the work."

"You've been working. Want to try me in wrestling?"

"Not really. I'm a good twenty ponds more than you."

"And stronger too. I don't doubt it. But you could not wrestle me."

"I wouldn't beat you in a race, I agree. But come on, wrestling?"

I stood up and waved him to his feet. "Just try it out. Give it a minute. A minute is a long time in wrestling. Give it a few seconds."

Dan-Boy got up slowly. He did not want to do this. He was not afraid of losing; he just did not want to do it. Of course, since he had never wrestled, he did not even know what to expect. I bent down in the way I liked to start a match. It was a little showmanship on my part, not for Dan-Boy, but whenever I wrestled. Dan-Boy made a sound to show he thought it silly. This was going to be too easy.

"This is my sport. I have the advantage. I'll let you put a hold on me. Any hold you want."

Dan-Boy did not know what to do. He grabbed both my wrists. I told him to say "go" when he was ready. He squeezed my wrists before he said "go." His inept hold might have illustrated his discomfort with the personal grappling associated with wrestling. I wanted to suggest something better, but he had accepted the challenge and would have to pay the price. I levered my arms simultaneously in the direction of his fingers and was out of his grip in the first second. While he marveled that his power had not been more effective on his bony opponent, I drove into him with my shoulder, like a football tackle. I would never have done this in a match, but in a match no one would have stood up straight and still as he was doing. He had not been ready to move fast. Maybe he could not move fast. He might have hit the ground uncomfortably hard. Falling backward is the hard way to go. Of course I put as much of my weight as I could on his chest and wrapped an arm around the back of his neck. He was strong enough to protect himself from a pin by bridging with me on him, but he did not know the concept. My arm reached all the way behind him and my weight shifted to his neck, not in a way that choked him but in a way that kept him pinned, even though his hands and legs were free. He flopped like a giant insect pinned on a board. I counted a slow one-two-three and let him up.

"Maybe you needed to get the feel of it. Want to try again? We haven't used a full minute yet."

Dan-Boy was angry. He brushed himself off and softly called me the worst names he could find. They reflected the agricultural background of the area where he was raised. I suddenly remembered how he had reacted to the beating at the school dance. It had hurt his pride a great deal. I wanted to say "It's just a game, a sport. There is more to it than being strong," or something more consoling if only I could find the words, but he stalked off as far as our little campsite would allow. At least he did not go off into the bush on his own. I was still confused about his reaction. I thought he was into sports; it would imply he had experience in losing; we all did. But then I thought: building his muscles were not like the sports I had done. Oh, I did not want to analyze it. He would get over it. But he never did. We were never close again. And I regretted this. I had no war buddy to call up at Christmas and share the latest developments in our lives, no important character from the start of adulthood to introduce to my wife, no friend who would grow out his hair to protest the culture of the generation that had controlled us. It was too late to find a new buddy. I had not even realized I wanted one. It was another disappointment from my Vietnam War.

As it turned out, I may have learned something that day, or in the subsequent days when I saw Dan-Boy was not going to forgive me. I may have grown up a measurable amount. It is a fact that I was careful from then on to today not to humiliate my friends. It did not actually serve my ego to pick the thing I could do best and press my friends into doing that thing. Every day Dan-Boy had looked upon me he saw that I was not good at the thing he did best and it did not hurt me a bit to have him think that way.

Sometimes I am asked if the War helped me to grow up. I always answer that I spent a year doing something outside my normal life and that doing something else as different might have taught me more. I could not deny I had grown up some in that year but I did not want to describe myself as needing maturity. Society had decided I was mature enough to kill somebody, even to decide whom to kill within certain parameters. Never again in my life would I be granted as much responsibility. I do not think I used it well although I think I used it as well as society demanded.

Our Mission was to end on our fourth day out. In the morning of that day, I went over with Leon, Ray, and Dan-Boy the route we should have taken. Loran and Ralph stood guard. Then I went over it with them while Leon and Dan-Boy stood guard. We went over our plan, and where we "had" to deviate from it. We talked about the terrain and the weather when we were various places. I tried to

make it like a movie in their memories. I put in little
incidents that had "occurred while we were there" and put
them to a location. We did not see much risk in our lie.
No one expected any of us to be especially articulate in
describing or remembering the trip. We had called in
anything we thought mattered as we "found" it and there was
nothing significant in any of it. The villages we "searched
and cleared" were not likely to complain about our story.
When we were sent out with no more expertise than mine,
the Captain should not have expected much. It might have
been that which bothered me the most: that we were sent
into a war zone without any real hope of accomplishing
anything, no matter how defined, other than getting a few
days closer to DROS, for us and for the Captain.

He had acted as if he were doing me a favor and an
honor. He was right that my ambitions in life were higher
than when I fell into the Army. I saw the prospects for these
American boys, young men without distinction, and I saw I
was one with them out here. Their prospects were my
prospects unless I took better advantage of my privileges.
But he was not right that I saw leading my colleagues into
the Vietnamese boonies as a step up. My higher ambition
was to get out of Vietnam with all my body parts. If my
previously bruised honor suffered no further injury, so
much the better.

I thought it would take about four hours to get us to
our evacuation point so we left camp before the day had
heated up with the idea of getting back before the mess hall
closed down for lunch. We would keep a hard pace getting
to the chopper so we would feel just a little more as if we
had been beating the bush for all four days. We already
fully looked and smelled the part. I took point on the first

leg, mainly to set the pace even though we all knew we would be pressing harder than usual. The first hour was merely invigorating. We were filled with the thought of cooked chow and a few days back at the base. We took our water break at 9:15. Five minutes was enough I thought.

Neon Leon was next on point. With his country background, he was the most used to the bush and he liked being up front. He had been there a lot and we generally felt good about having him there. But he was smiling too much during our break and I knew he was thinking about pushing the pace even harder. I went up front before we moved out and talked a bit to calm him down. I told him our little deception was not extraordinary and we should regard the whole trip as normal business. Lunch would be around when we got back to base. No one would care if we cleaned ourselves up first. I suggested we were ahead of schedule and he should remember that we were still in the bush of Vietnam so we should put caution first. I know I said these things to him and that I did not think at the time he needed to hear them, just that I believed in caution and was being cautious myself by making the speech. And I remember very well my tone. I was comradely. We were not close and I wanted him to listen to me. I did not think he would respond to anything from me that looked like exerting authority. I was just talking, advising. "OK, Neon. For the next hour, you're the man. Be the man." I wore down his smile and patted him on the back as he set out. I stood in the same spot as the others went by and patted each of them too. It made me feel more of a leader. It felt good but I would not be intoxicated by it.

I had stepped into the end of our line of march less than five minutes when I heard the shot. It was followed immediately by the rustling sound of everyone dropping to the ground. Then it was quiet. This bunch was experienced enough and disciplined enough to hold their return fire until they had a target. I just wanted to pull out, but here was a chance to file something real into our trip report. Lying flat as possible on the ground does not let anyone see who fired the shot. "Stay down" I said loud enough the whole squad would hear me, and then worked my way up the line and asked each of them what he heard. When I got to Dan-Boy, I did not like his answer. He said he thought Neon was hit. I crawled up to Neon. He was moaning to himself. I did not think he was undisciplined enough to make noise so I worried his low moans represented some loss of consciousness. I slid up beside him. "My leg," he said. I saw right away he had not been shot. A round had run up through his boot, hit a bone, and spun around inside his leg. It had come back out, I judged from the bloody hole in his pants near his crotch. Like all young men, I particularly worried what damage it might have done to his family jewels.

It was a booby trap, a cheap, hand-made one. He had stepped on something that triggered the round. We had seen these before in our AO. They usually came in large groups. "Mine-field," I called back to Dan-Boy. I almost said "Pass it on," but I knew he would, that everyone would. I looked for the booby trap to see if there was anything about it I could tell the others to look for. The hole for it was five feet behind Neon. He must have taken a step before falling forward. It was a tin can with some metal bits inside. It had been covered with leaves, invisible when Neon hit it. We were not on any trail so there was no way to know where the rest of them were. I told Dan-Boy to follow the track I made crawling up to Leon from the back and to take the others back the same way. "Low crawl," I ordered. Maybe I had passed over one and not set it off because I never had all my weight on it.

I cut Neon's pant leg off and put a bandage on the exit point first. That is where most of the blood was coming out. I used the bandage on his belt and then removed his boot and bandaged the entry wound with the kit on my belt. It was obvious the bandages were not going to help much. His leg was torn up inside and no bandage would affect that. He needed surgery fast. I heard another shot and a yelp. Someone else was hit. Loran swore loudly. The vigor in his voice was a good sign. Then he said he was hit but it was okay, he could go on. He concluded with some unkind words for Charlie.

"Neon, you're patched up for now. Let's get the medevac. We're in close radio range. They'll be here quick. But we got to get away from the booby traps. Can you help me?" I dragged him by the shoulders and he pushed with his good leg until we were 15 feet back along my original track. It was not working. We were pressing hard on every square inch. So I picked him up in a fireman's carry and went back to where the others were gathered. A quick look at Loran showed he had put his hand on a mine. It had a bloody hole in it that Ralph was bandaging. I thought the bones had been hit; it was a mess but not bleeding much. I picked up Neon again and turned to the squad. "Charlie may have stayed around his traps. He might have heard 'em go off. Grab Neon's pack. Spread out. Follow me." I had used the infantry slogan without irony.

I did not want to take the time to transfer my load to anyone else. Besides, the man-carry was my best event in training. Ray jogged beside me to get Neon's pack off; less weight for me. We had to go where Charlie did not expect us to go. If he was waiting, he would have already looked over the area and thought about our retreat. I went uphill. Leon was not heavy this day.

He was my responsibility. For all my claims that I was not a leader, I had taken the job, and the others accepted me in it. In the field is not the time to parse the meaning of roles. They were all my responsibility. I did not feel responsible for the mission but this was *my* team. I went as far as I could until my legs were too shaky to be safe for Neon and me. By then we were away from the booby traps anyway. I sat down and laid out Neon as comfortably as I could. I spread the others out to guard. Ralph stuck beside me with the radio.

"Ralph, we gotta call in but right now I am not that sure where we are. And, Ralph, we are not where we are supposed to be."

Ralph did not answer. His attention was on Neon. As a radio man, he was used to carrying the load, not contributing to the message. I had some idea of where we were. I had tried to pay attention to direction during our scramble but I was not exactly sure where we were when Neon got hit. I was sure of the direction to take, not where we were along it. I had led a route different than the way we came in so we would all have a feeling of seeing more, of going farther, not four days-worth, but more than the one day we had actually travelled. But even if I knew where we were, I needed to find a place where the chopper could come in. We were on a steep slope without any clearing nearby. Neon was conscious but bleeding heavily.

I was thinking ahead now, feeling sharp mentally. While my thighs recovered from our burst up the mountain, all my energy was focused in my brain. Ship navigators in the days of sail had found islands with only dead reckoning to guide them for days. Our lives hung no less in the balance than theirs had. I mentally retraced our steps from the morning departure. I needed to concentrate. Tending to Neon was taking up mental energy. There was nothing any of us could do for him. I let him out of my mind for a few minutes.

I sat back and stared at the map, seeing not the heavy creased and stained, plastic-covered paper in front of me but the bush we had traversed. All morning I had been too relaxed, thinking we were getting out, but I had some good habits from my time here. I did not look at the beauty of the land or the curiosity of nature as I did back in the world. I had looked constantly for signs of Charlie. There was that slope where someone behind me slid noisily and I had halted to wait for any responding sounds in the forest. We were probably a click and a half out at that point. I could visualize the shadows at the moment of that wait. Our route was north of east then. I could not see the place on the map, but I knew where it should be. There was a small stream where I considered going to its source to be sure it would be safe to drink, but decided it was too big and the spring likely too far out of our way. I had adjusted the direction then for the next point. It was Ray. I thought of him as we went on from there and visualized how he was following the terrain. I had been pleased at how he did not cut through the saddle that was right on our route. That would have been a good place for an ambush. The saddle might have been a certain place I could find on the map.

And so on until I felt I might have us located. Even if I did, however, it still did not help me know what to do.

It was still no good. I could not grasp the moment as I needed to do. I reviewed the situation rapidly and focused on what was inside myself. I felt beads of sweat on my brow, escaping every once in a while to drip down my face, I could hardly wipe them away. My sleeve was rolled up, my bare arm was dripping of its own excretions. A ring of mosquito bites burned along my neck. I heard Loran squirming with the tension built up in him, the leaves under him made a gentle swishing. He was not breaking any twigs in his nervous discomfort so his sounds were not reaching far. There were no sounds of birds and I wondered if that was due to the time of day, our sterile location, their fear of our presence or of Charlie's. I was monitoring the sounds in the bush. I cut those off. I had to trust the rest of the squad.

I was smart. I knew it; smart as any of the officers. I was a screw-up and a lazy ingrate, but I was smart and I had to find a way out of here while Neon was still alive. Another thought was stealing my attention and I had to drop it too. The idea that my scam to make it an easy trip, or maybe just a safe one, had to be admitted. Let them find us where we should not have been. I did not know what they would do to me. This was not the time to speculate on their options. Whatever it was, it would not be worse than losing Neon out here. A look toward him touched me deeply and I felt tears forming. I had not cried in ten years. He looked terrible. A pool of his blood was staining the jungle under him. The thought flashed through that I might be seen as a resister in the war, a public figure representing my generation. But not if Neon were lost. My mind was trying to make this something heroic and I stopped it. This was only an attempt to get us home again. Any resistance to the war had to be done before getting here or after leaving here.

Ralph was whispering to me. He wanted orders. He knew who I was and that I did not know what to do but he still wanted orders. "Sit tight, Ralph. I've getting a plan together. Just gimme one more minute." I ran to and climbed the tallest tree in the area. I climbed to where the remaining trunk bent toward the horizon with my weight. The tree was healthy and I swayed in it to get it to lift me even higher. Like a gift from the luck of my past, I saw a gap in the forest crown. It could be a clearing, a flat place where a chopper might fit. I took a bearing and dropped branch to branch like an orangutan headed to the ground for a quick drink of water. "Call us in, Ralph."

I told them we were off course. They did not ask why. I told them we needed a medevac. I gave them the coordinates of the possible LZ. We would be there when the chopper arrived. Even if it was not a clearing, we would pop some smoke[60] and get Neon out, maybe Loran too.

I called in the squad, leaving no guard out for a few moments. I told them our story was changed. The new version was this: on Day 1, I had told them our mission was to hang out on this mountain and observe. They had not agreed to anything but to follow my orders. Everything else was just as it actually occurred. No one argued. I told them we had about a click to our LZ. Then I sent out a guard while Dan-Boy and I built a field-expedient[61] stretcher using

---

[60] Set off a grenade of colored smoke to show location.
[61] I.e., improvised in the field.

the shirts from everyone in the squad tied between two poles separated by forked branches.

Neon was unconscious when we loaded him on it. Dan-Boy took the front while Ray and Ralph took the back. I carried the radio and led the way. Loran had to bring up the back and I worried that if he dropped out we would lose him, but there was no other way to arrange things. I took the most direct route down the slope. It was a mistake. Dan-Boy took the stretcher behind me and they got going too fast. Someone tripped or just gave out and Leon was spilled onto the rocks. When I got back to him, they had rolled him face up and were getting him back on the stretcher.

"He hit soft. Nothing was broken there. He'll be alright. We gotta go slower is all." Ray was chattering. It must have been he who dropped his end. Dan-Boy was silently angry, too tired to complain. I rotated the tasks. I took the front of the stretcher. Ralph took the radio and the lead. Ray stayed on the rear. I asked for a pace the group could manage. Dan-Boy had been too aggressive. He had worn out himself and led to the drop as much as Ray. I could sense his blame falling on me when he should have been looking within himself. Or maybe he had to go too fast since I was getting ahead of them. The blame belonged with me for a lot of it, but not for dropping Leon. The blame might channel up the line to the Captain and the Secretary of Defense and Johnson and Nixon and the voters, but for the moment, the blame did not matter.

The chopper could not land and they could not see a workable LZ nearby so they hauled Leon's limp body up on a basket. Then they took Loran up. He was looking weak at that point. He uttered no complaint.

The medevac had advertised our location pretty clearly to the whole countryside so the rest of us were anxious to move out. The chopper gave us a new exit point. We had a good two clicks to go if we could find it straightaway. We went fast now, our injured were off. Charlie did not show up. We got a little lost going to the LZ, but the next chopper talked us in via radio and we got out in good order.

Two casualties was a bad score for a squad-sized mission. The only positive in it was the minefield we discovered constituted intelligence so we were seen as accomplishing something. The officers who debriefed us were sympathetic. They did not press us for explanations of what we could not explain well. There were no accusations. They barely asked why we did not do our assignment. They really only showed concern for the incidents at the end, which they felt we handled as well as we could. No one offered us any Bronze Stars. Two Purple Hearts was all we had earned.

Neon never went back to English. They took him directly to a better hospital somewhere, maybe Phu Cat, the Air Force base. We always thought of it as the best accommodations within a chopper flight. We were told he made it back to the States but we never heard how messed up he was. Loren was in the LZ English field hospital for a few days where we visited him and the officers interviewed him. Then he went back to the States and lost contact with us. We imagined he had a full recovery and got a quiet job in a small town and went to the bar on Saturday night and got fat even before he found his beautiful, tolerant, full-figured wife.

XXXV: Close Out

Little by little, my DROS came closer. On the outside, nothing was changing. I was already fully acclimated, casual about my situation, cognizant of and confident about what I had to do every invariable day. My last mission ended two days before I was to fly out. We got back in before dark and went to an immediate debriefing. I skipped chow and went to the club.

There was a band playing; all girls. They were Korean and very polished performers. One of them did a number wearing balloons which she popped as the song went on. It was less of a tease than it sounds because she was wearing a glitzy two-piece outfit under the balloons that showed a lot of skin and no sexuality. The show was too plastic. We had lived a gritty reality and I could not pretend she was exciting for me. I did not know what sex was like exactly, but it was not like her. I watched the show closely, hoping to feel inspired, but it just did not come to me. Maybe it was the singing. At least they did not do country; it was American pop but not my kind of pop; no soul, no Mo-Town, no throwback be-bop, no Jersey cool, no British working class ennui, no folk-rock gentleness, and not even any of the electric rock that I could hardly stand. What's left? Just bubblegum, I guess. They broke local tradition and did not even close with the Vietnam anthem: I Gotta Get Outta of This Place by the Animals. I could not know if they were obeying the Army directive that the song could not be performed or if they just thought it too raucous for their program. Nonetheless, I watched the show as intently as anyone. It would be my last in the Nam. They displayed good musical craftsmanship and watching the body of any fit young female in minimal clothing was entertaining.

Just after it ended Mai came to my table. "Churchkey, you looking very hard at those balloons."

"No Mai, I was watching the drummer. I never saw a girl on drums but she was very good, don't you think?"

Mai may have noticed I did not look at her as I spoke. She stood before me and waited until I looked up. "What is wrong, Churchkey? You look sad tonight."

"Damn Mai, are you perceptive! I am feeling blue. You know what DROS means?"

"I know. How many days you have left? Too many, right?"

"Too few." She looked at me with genuine curiosity. No one ever said that.

Mai looked at me directly, right through my eyes.

"So why you sad? You want to stay Vietnam?"

"I am sad, Mai, because I must leave the most interesting woman I ever met."

"You don't know me, Churchkey."

"I wish I did, Mai. But then, you don't know me and if you did, you would know I am very ordinary."

"You have time. You do not want to know me."

"I guess you are right, Mai. I wanted to know you and to do things with you and see things but we cannot do that here."

"We could do that. What is stopping us? We talk. It is not always about the Army. I'm not in the Army. I just work here. Most of the day I'm not here."

Her face was so beautiful I could hardly stand to hold her in view. She was another life form from the girls at school. There had never been a girl in America so beautiful, no face on a magazine cover or in a movie held this perfection. Her slender body belonged in a church, proof there was a God that something so exquisite could exist. Her only fault was in showing any interest in me.

"Do you have a boyfriend out there in Vietnam, Mai?"

"I told you before; I have no boyfriend. There are no good boys in my village. You don't listen to me?"

"I heard you, Mai. I wish I could stay in Vietnam but only after the war. I hate to be in the Army."

"You won't be back after the war."

"Yes. I did not mean to say I would come back. Just that I wish the war was over. Then I could be here."

"You will not stay. You do not want to stay. You will not come back. There is always war in Vietnam."

She was wrong, of course, on that last point but closer to the truth than I knew at the time. There had been war there continuously since before her birth or mine, and would be war for a long time to come as well. My four-year war prediction was not as pessimistic as I thought.

I was enjoying, in some kind of masochistic way, the idea of having a life with Mai. I had forbidden myself from thinking of this but on my last couple days in country it seemed safe enough. I tried to find words to explain that she would not want to live in the United States with me or any GI. She would be too isolated by language and culture. She would be disappointed in me to see that I am not as outstanding as I appeared to be among enlisted GIs. I could be trainee-of-the-cycle but needed to change something significant in myself to be a college graduate. Back in America, she would be too beautiful to be with me. Everyone would think I was with her only for that, for sex, and I wondered if they might be right. How long would it

take for her to see me as that shallow? I saw some kind of security in knowing I was not good looking, that she was not interested in me for reasons so superficial, that is, if she were interested in me. It was not fair of me to consider the possibility that she would abandon me for a better partner. She had never shown any dishonesty. What I most admired about her may have been how disengaged she was from the immediate gratification world around us. GIs counted the days until we returned but we largely lived as if there were no tomorrow. It was glamorous for us to care so little.

If she committed to me, I should not doubt her. ...I would never know if she really would commit to me. I could not imagine what it would take to find out. Then I remembered I was a soldier, a category that required courage of a sort. I had some experience in sucking it up and going ahead regardless of the risks.

"Mai, would you go to America with me if there were a way to do that?"

"I see lots of GI here. Every night one of them want to take me to America."

"Am I just the same as all of them, Mai? I do not feel the same."

"You are not the same. You are a good man. You serious? You want to take me to America or you just ask so you can think about it?"

"Five and a wake-up. That means I leave here the day after tomorrow. One more day; I have just one more day here."

Mai stood very still for a few seconds and then slowly nodded her head. Without looking at me, she reached into her pocket and took out something which she put on the bar under her hand. I heard her say quietly but very distinctly, "Please leave club now and do not come back tomorrow." Then she went through a noisy beaded curtain to a room behind her, leaving no one to tend bar. On the bar was the wooden bottle opener I had carved. My courage was used up. I did as she said.

XXXVI: Departure

At the airport, we were searched thoroughly for drugs or gold. Some of the soul brothers had longish hair at this point and the guards ran their fingers through it to be sure nothing was hidden there. They found Afro combs and pencils. They did not do body cavity searches. I was glad I had not secreted a bayonet or any other contraband, but by then I was not likely to challenge the Army on anything. I did not have any urge to carry back a souvenir: no cigarette lighter with my unit crest, no tattoo saying "Born to Kill," no heroin habit, no shrapnel in my skull, no child conceived in momentary passion, no hatred of an Asian race, no fear of sudden sounds, no lifelong dedication to those unfortunate brothers who had stood beside me and protected me with every fiber and sinew in their young, muscular, battered bodies.

We stopped in Tokyo airport to refuel. I bought Asian-themed gifts in the airport shops for my family: brass candle-stick holders, a calendar with pictures of bamboo in each season, a miniature radio, a ceramic panda. I had plenty of money. I was not making much in the Army. My monthly take-home pay was only two digits until I was promoted, but I was not spending anything at all. It was the most money I had ever saved. With the GI Bill to help pay for college, I could use my savings to buy a car. All those savings soon went for a used, gray MGB. Those cars were hard to start in the cold but they rode low and looked good.

I was given two weeks leave after a couple days at Ft. Campbell, Kentucky to get a haircut and recover from jet lag. Uncle Sam gave me a plane ticket home, but it was written as a military order and required that I wear my uniform out into the world. I was worried about that... no not worried, interested in the reaction of civilians to my uniform. The world seemed very different than before. I had been away a year and a half, counting training time, but that was very long in my experience. I heard a little about Woodstock which took place in August, a few months before my DROS, and I suspected, hoped, it expressed the culture of my peers. I heard plans for the march in Washington in November that year, a bigger version of the one in 1968. I did not understand much about it but I was encouraged that my peers were being heard and discouraged they might not see themselves as my peers. It was hard to be a hippie with my hair and clothes. News about the My Lai massacre first leaked out in November although it had occurred exactly 18 months earlier, back when I was still in school. Would people confront me on the street? If they did, what would I do? I would not be angry with them. They probably knew more about My Lai than I did. They knew more about the music and styles that were current. I longed to be them judging me instead of me judging myself.

At LaGuardia Airport, I found a bus to Penn Station. No one gave me a glance except for two privates whose lack of insignia told me they were just trainees. I nodded in their direction. As a Spec 4, I did not have significant rank, but they could see I was well out of training. They could have been on home leave before taking Tiger Airlines across the Pacific. At Penn Station, no one gave me a glance. I had to wait for two hours, during which I read the New York Times and tried hard not to look up at the civilians. New Yorkers had seen the likes of me too much to care about one more of us. There were no college girls around to impress but there were plenty of black people of

all ages. I had become used to being around the brothers--
most of my unit was black—but I was not used to black
people of other generations and gender.

I called my parents from a phone booth and told
them when I would get home. They would like the
uniform. They had not seen me in one before. They would
both see the inadequacy of my rank, that I was not an
officer, but my father would appreciate that I had done what
I was asked to do by my country and my mother would be
pleased that my head and all four limbs were attached.

I got on the bus to Connecticut and it was only half
full but a boy, probably not yet ten years old, got up to offer
me his seat in case I wanted to sit there. I smiled and
declined. He came up to me a minute later with his smaller
brother and asked if he could touch my insignia. I shook
his hand as his mother came running up the aisle to grab her
boys. She apologized for bothering me. A middle-aged
couple waited for me when we exited the bus to thank me
for my service. I began to think I might know something
more than these people who had access to the daily
newspaper for the past year.

The taxi driver took me home, twenty minutes
without a word until we got to my driveway. Bridgeport was
less sophisticated than New York, but he had seen a full
share of twenty-year olds in uniform. He probably knew
someone who had been to Vietnam. He was not of the
Woodstock generation.

He would not accept any payment from me, just
said simply that he owed me more than I owed him
although the meter read more than my bus fare had cost
from New York to Bridgeport.